The Man Who Hated Emily Brontë

Previously Published Work

Cape Breton Is the Thought Control Centre of Canada, 1969

Lord Nelson Tavern, 1974

Century, 1986

A Night at the Opera, 1992

The Man Who Loved Jane Austen, 1999

The Man Who Hated Emily Brontë

⚜ ⚜ ⚜

Ray Smith

The Porcupine's Quill

National Library of Canada Cataloguing in Publication

Smith, Ray, 1941–
The man who hated Emily Brontë/Ray Smith.

ISBN 0-88984-245-0

1. Title.

PS8587.M583M363 2004   C813´.54   C2004-900988-5

1 2 3 4 • 06 05 04

Published by The Porcupine's Quill,
68 Main Street, Erin, Ontario N0B 1T0.
www.sentex.net/˜pql

Readied for the press by John Metcalf; copy edited by Doris Cowan.

This is a work of fiction. Any resemblance of characters to persons,
living or dead, is purely coincidental.

Represented in Canada by the Literary Press Group.
Trade orders are available from University of Toronto Press.

We acknowledge the support of the Ontario Arts Council
and the Canada Council for the Arts for our publishing program.
The financial support of the Government of Canada
through the Book Publishing Industry Development Program
is also gratefully acknowledged. Thanks, also
to the Government of Ontario through the Ontario
Media Development Corporation's Ontario Book Initiative.

Canada Council   Conseil des Arts
for the Arts   du Canada

Canadä

ONTARIO ARTS COUNCIL
CONSEIL DES ARTS DE L'ONTARIO

For Nicholas and Alexander

'Idle tales you'll say, and so say I.'
Emily Brontë, *Wuthering Heights*

———❧———

All chapter epigraphs are also
from *Wuthering Heights*

One

An erect and handsome figure – and rather morose.

The canine … was sneaking wolfishly to the back of my legs, her lip curled up, and her white teeth watering for a snatch.

I began to dream almost before I became sensible of my locality.

2001 – I have just returned from a visit to my landlady, who is also my department chairperson. When she confirmed by telephone last week that I was hired, she added that her basement apartment was available. The rent sounded reasonable. Just before noon today, I arrived in Montreal and cabbed from the airport. Her house is in posh Westmount, about halfway up the mountain. Teaching obviously pays well in Quebec. With this promise of wealth beguiling my imagination, I climbed the steps to the Scottish baronial portico and rang the doorbell.

The distant chime summoned a yipping ball of fur followed by an Amazon with black eyes suspicious beneath a heavy swatch of black hair. The dog sniffed my feet and yipped.

'Ms Heidi Felsen?' I said.

A nod was the answer.

'Will Franklyn, your new tenant, ma'am. I hope I haven't inconvenienced you by arriving too early?'

One hand held a coffee cup; the other hand, once she had the door open, returned to holding her robe shut, but not quickly enough to prevent the revelation of two considerable mounds of bosom.

She shrugged.

'If you'd been too early I wouldn't have answered the door. Wait there, I'll get the key. Stay, Tinker Bell.'

She walked off along the hall into a murmur of subdued jazz

« 9 »

piano. A fabulous dragon in multicoloured needlework ramped over the shoulders of her black silk robe. I thought it odd that she left me in the vestibule with the dog guarding me, but assumed that, like me, she values her splendid isolation.

The vestibule and the bit of hall I could see beyond were spacious and bright. A poster for something called La Galerie de l'Art de l'Âme de la Nation hung on the wall beside me; I was trying with indifferent success to translate the French text when Ms Felsen returned.

'Stay, Tinker Bell. Tinks is a Yorkshire terrier, a sweet dog, she won't bother you.' She led me back down the steps and along the side of the house. 'You have your own entrance,' she remarked as she unlocked the door. 'It's very cosy.'

She waved vaguely at a couch, a dresser, a nasty chrome and plastic table with two questionable chairs, a kitchen nook with fridge and stove.

Cosy meant tiny.

'The bathroom is in there. The couch opens out for your bed. Bed and bath linen in the closet here, and you can use the washer and dryer in the back of the main basement, through that door there.'

'I'll take it.'

'You'll want groceries, I expect. Do you know Montreal?'

'No, I grew up in Nova Scotia – I've never been here before.'

'The nearest supermarket is down the hill to Sherbrooke and right four or five blocks. Turn the fridge on now and it'll be cold when you get back. Come and see me later and I'll fill you in on the job.'

Back with some basic groceries, I had a sandwich and explored my new home. China and cutlery for two, a bare sufficiency of mixing bowls and pots, a toaster and a microwave. With only the window in the door, another beside it and the small one in the bathroom, it is dark. It is also quiet – I can barely hear the music from above, footsteps are muted, and the occasional murmur of conversation is indistinct. I will have all the splendid isolation I can desire.

While washing up, I reflected on the unlikely circumstances which had landed me here. Ms Felsen's evident business-like sanity comes as something of a surprise, for, entirely illogically, I had been judging all Montrealers, or at least all Montreal women, by the whimsical eccentricity of Gudrun Sigurdardóttir, a more-or-less Montrealer with whom I spent a possibly incautious weekend during a conference in Aarhus, Denmark. In the agreeable Casablanca bar, we had absorbed perhaps a few too many glasses of Ceres Royal beer, when Gudrun insisted I should apply for a job at the Montreal junior college where she taught.

'They won't hire an unknown by e-mail.'

'They will when they find out at the last minute that I'm staying here another year, and then three of the geriatrics will retire and you'll be permanent. I know – I am a seeress, a völva in Icelandic. And don't look at me like that – it's a different word entirely.'

'Well ...'

'And the department head has a basement apartment you might be able to rent. That's where I lived.'

'Perhaps I'll just try to get the job first.'

'You're going to love Montreal,' she insisted, 'because it's full of bars just like this.'

'And women just like you?'

'No women are just like me,' she replied, smiling and screwing up her chocolate-brown eyes, 'but there are lots of babes in Montreal if that's what you want.'

Following Gudrun's instructions, I waited until August to e-mail my CV and application to Ms Felsen, and against all odds here I am. And Gudrun ...

But nothing more of Gudrun now.

My clothes stowed away and the above account typed, I lay on the couch to read. In ten minutes I slipped into a welcome slumber.

I found myself drifting in a dream of two rounded glacier mountains. A monstrous dog yipped atop one mountain, while a multicoloured dragon ramped about the other. Then Gudrun was astride the dragon's back – 'I am an Icelandic vulva and I told you so!' she cried. Shapes loomed grotesquely out of the shadows. Hums and whirrs touched the air ...

Was that a tapping at the window? No, surely not.

I struggled toward consciousness into the subterranean twilight.

The hum came from the refrigerator, others from deeper in the building.

The building was a house ... in Montreal ... Ms Felsen's house.

Suddenly, running footsteps above, a second set of footsteps, now on the level, now on stairs.

What now?

A low, unearthly scream, strangely muffled, at the window, then penetrating the very walls, filling the world, not a scream of horror or terror, but a melancholic keening, such a scream, perhaps, as one might have heard floating above the moors and crags of Wuthering Heights ...

Running feet, screams, screams of indistinguishable words, syllables, the slam of a door, more keening.

I rather think I heard, 'Come back, oh my heart's darling.'

Possibly Ms Felsen lives less graciously than I at first surmised. I decided to defer my visit until later.

Two

A decidedly shabby upper garment.

Her position before was sheltered from the light; now, I had a distinct view of her whole figure and countenance. She was slender: ... an admirable form, and the most exquisite little face that I have ever had the pleasure of beholding.

In the absence of clear proofs of his condition, I deemed it best to abstain from noticing his curious conduct.

With my sleep disordered, I was awake at five this morning. I puttered about until seven. When by eight I heard no movement from Ms Felsen above, I decided to stroll over to the college instead, hoping to find her there at some time during the day. Classes don't start for three days, but I could do some of the paperwork.

I found the building readily enough, perched on a bit of an eminence on the side of the hill, surrounded by broad, sloping lawns shaded by fully grown maples, oaks and even elms. It is a large, handsome edifice done, like Ms Felsen's home, like so many older buildings in the neighbourhood, in Scottish baronial style, with turrets, battlements, crenellations and arrow windows. With a wary glance for a raised portcullis, I pulled open the great oaken door and stepped into the gloom of the entrance hall. The lady in the porter's booth appeared not to have been carousing till the second cock, and readily enough directed me toward the English department office.

Although the medieval tone was dispelled within by fluorescent-lit hallways, institutional beige walls and modern doors, the layout of halls and stairs retained an authentic irregularity and eccentricity, so that several times I had to ask my way. Nonetheless, I soon found myself before a counter greeting a young woman who was talking on the telephone, scrabbling though papers with her left hand and

« 13 »

clicking the mouse with her right. She managed to squeeze in a request that I identify myself and my business; after three or four tries I slipped through a narrow window of her attention with my name, and got in return a slip of paper with the message 'Go to HRA. Your office – C2304' and a wave of her hand along the hall.

Asking her for more detail was obviously pointless, so I wandered along the hall looking for help.

Through a nearby office door I espied a woman silhouetted against the window. She appeared preoccupied and I was turning away, but she must have sensed my presence.

'Can I help you?'

The lights were not on, and her silhouette was made even darker by a long-sleeved black blouse and black hair.

'Perhaps. I find this place confusing, and the secretary is too busy to explain. Can you please tell me where to find C2304?'

'You're new.'

'Will Franklyn, at your service.'

'Margaret Taylor. Yes, Tracy is always busy at the beginning of term. The office you want is the third door along on this side.'

'Well, thank you.'

An open door revealed a handsome but dishevelled man in his fifties, resting comfortably in a swivel armchair, so comfortably indeed that he was asleep. I went back to the woman. She was now seated with the desk light on, and I saw that she is quite good-looking.

'Excuse me again – my officemate is busy and ...'

'Your officemate is asleep.'

'Resting his eyes.'

'Exemplary discretion. What can I do for you?'

'What and where is HRA?'

'Human Resources Access – adminspeak for the Personnel Department – along the hallway to your right, then left, then ask someone.'

'Thank you again.'

In time I found it. Forms were presented for me to fill out. By noon I had been run through a warren of offices, and had supplied most of the obligatory fodder to the administrative beast, receiving in return an office key and a mailbox key. After coffee and a sandwich in a small cafeteria, I made my way back to my office, where I discovered the dishevelled man still asleep.

'Asleep!' he exclaimed in response to my cough. 'Of course not. I was resting my eyes.'

'Exactly what I thought.'

'How long have I been resting my eyes?'

'Since just after nine when I passed by the first time.'

He considered this groggily, then glanced at his watch.

'Noon thirty! Who are you, the Slumber Sheriff? The Sleep Police dismisseth us?'

'Will Franklyn, your new officemate.'

He looked at me doubtfully.

'Ensign Ass, more likely. As we don't hire able-bodied white males, and you have no wheelchair, are you perhaps deaf or dumb? No, evidently not. Blind?'

'Not the last time I looked.'

'Perhaps blindness came on when you weren't looking. How many heads do I have?'

'One.'

'Wrong – two, but an understandable error. The second head is only visible to students, administrators and some of my colleagues. Are you a poufter?'

'Not so far as I've been able to tell.'

'Can't be that, then. Rules one, three and five: *More poufters*. Single father?'

'Not to my knowledge.'

'Then you're either a refugee or mad.'

'Given the choice, I'll take refugee.'

'As I'm mad, I recommend madness, but choose as you wish. Refugee from where?'

'Doctoral studies at the University of Alberta.'

He stared at me, aghast.

'Spare me the sordid details.'

'And a recent year at Edinburgh.'

'That's better. However, all that matters is that you made it out apparently intact of life and limb.'

'I barely made it here. Very confusing building.'

'Give it thirty years.'

'I got directions from a woman in black a few offices along. Margaret ... something.'

'Taylor. A maiden fair to see, the pearl of minstrelsy. Hired two or three years ago. Known as the Black Death, the Black Widow or the Black Orchid.'

'The Black Death? Isn't that a bit rough? I saw she was wearing black, but ...'

'She slays all men.'

'Not for me, you mean.'

'Rich man, poor man, beggarman, thief, she lays waste them all.'

'All?' I asked meaningfully.

'Don't be pedantic, Ensign Ass. Dr Taylor is a former student of mine and despite the nicknames a dear friend. I mean that the Black Death worked by random selection, and although it brought them down indiscriminately, it only dropped half the population, so you may be safe.'

He brightened up.

'Now, which desk do you want? This one is mine.'

'I envy you your taste.' It was a handsome double pedestal in mahogany near the window. 'But I had rather decided on the other one,' indicating the vile steel thing in a dark corner.

'An excellent choice. As for files, you can borrow the back half of the bottom drawer of my cabinet. And I think I can spare six inches or so of my bookcase. Or perhaps you'd prefer to use the floor?'

'The six inches will be more than enough.'

'As the actress said to the bishop. If you've been in grad school the past ten years, you've probably forgotten about books. How long will you take to forget everything you learned in grad school?'

'I'm not sure I ...'

'Yes, it's a bit early. But get to work on it. The sooner you forget all that, the sooner you can be sane, that is, mad, like all the rest of us.'

'I don't quite understand.'

'Of course you don't – this is Quebec. Never mind the why and wherefore, you will.'

'I ...'

'That's apt – "You Will." That was the name you offered, as I dimly recall. Yes, "Will Franklyn", you said. Chaucerian. You Will Franklyn, I Will Blake. At least I think I'm Will Blake today. Yesterday I was Will Shakespeare and the day before I was Emily Brontë. Nasty experience. Don't be Emily Brontë unless they force you. Emily Dickinson's not much fun either. Anyway, the Black Death is often Emily Brontë, even looks like her, but perhaps she'll spare her now and then. If you really want her.'

He regarded me doubtfully.

'Might you?'

'I don't have the figure.'

'Right. Stick to sane ones like Virginia Woolf or Sylvia Plath. But as you're fresh out of grad school, you probably think this is all silliness. Well, it is, because this is Quebec, that is, the real world, that is, the unreal world. You need a prophet, a seer, to see clearly here. Tiresias would do. Was Tiresias a man who became a woman or a woman who became a man?'

'A man who became a woman as I recall.'

'Evidently you're not Tiresias. Yet. Step back out the door and read the name plate.'

'Harrison Morgan,' I read.

'Thank God. Well, that's settled. And if you'd just sit down, you'd be settled too.'

'Well, I really should see if I can find Ms Felsen. Details about courses, schedule, students, grading, etc.'

'I can tell you all that. What do you most hate teaching?'

'Well, I'm a specialist in the Western Canadian novel.'

'That's out – you'll be doing remedial grammar. When do you most hate teaching?'

'Early morning.'

'You'll have all eight o'clocks. What sort of students would you like to have?'

'The usual sort – literate kids who enjoy novels.'

'You'll have 120 mouth-breathers who are intellectually challenged by the instructions on a chocolate bar wrapper.'

'Surely the students can't be ...'

'Oh no, most of them are good kids, much the same as the kids

Socrates had in Know Thyself, a.k.a. Wanking 101, but to get them you have to be here a while, or have compromising photographs of the executive.'

'I'd been thinking of buying a camera.'

'On second thought, don't bother. This is Quebec. Along with the usual venality and corruption, we have shoplifting cabinet ministers and union leaders, former terrorists on the bench, and legislators consorting with underage prostitutes. Of course, if *you* look the wrong way at a girl in class *you'll* lose your job.'

'Sounds pretty standard to me.'

'Good. You'll get along fine.'

From somewhere down the hall came a unearthly scream, strangely muffled, yet penetrating the very walls.

'That couldn't be Ms Felsen, could it?' I asked.

'Yes, comme d'habitude. I wouldn't bother her just now if I were you. Quite a babe, wouldn't you say?'

'She's certainly an imposing figure of a woman.'

'Imposing? Ambiguous but apt:

> '"You'll soon get used to her looks," said he,
> "And a very nice girl you will find her!
> She may very well pass for forty-three
>   In the dusk, with a light behind her!"'

'And speaking of ladies who've passed their best-before date, what do you think of the building?' spreading his arms to indicate the school.

'The style is a bit heavy on the outside; pleasant enough inside, I suppose.'

'Scottish baronial can be oppressive,' he agreed, 'but there's a certain whimsy in faux medieval castle motifs on a modern North American institute of higher learning. With sufficient supplies, a few determined scholars should have no trouble holding out against a horde of Highlanders armed with claymores, haggises, quaichs, gabions and such.'

'Do you mean it was purpose-built as a college?'

'Good grief, no, though I suppose it comes to the same thing – it was built as a lunatic asylum.'

Three

We at length arrived in the large, warm, cheerful apartment where I was formally received.

By way of ornament, three gaudily-painted canisters.

Perceiving myself in a blunder, I attempted to correct it.

Where is she – my amiable lady?

At home, through the late afternoon and early evening, I puzzled over college and ministerial descriptions of the courses I am to teach. If Harrison's picture of the students I can expect is correct, these directives are perhaps a mite optimistic, peppered as they are with references to correct spelling, punctuation, grammar, usage, vocabulary and rhetorical devices, all laying out original perceptions and well-constructed arguments. Indeed the documents themselves are not models of clarity. Oh well, I decided, over the years I have taught lots of students straight out of high school, and these are not likely to be much different.

All the while, I listened for evidence that Ms Felsen was home. At about six-thirty, muted music and footsteps were the necessary signals.

'You again?'

Tinker Bell yipped protectively.

'Excuse me, if another time is more convenient ... You mentioned I should see you if I had any questions and ...'

'Oh well, you might as well come in. I don't have long, I'm just going out.'

Evidently it was for a grander occasion than I'm used to, for she was wearing a black cocktail dress in a swishy material, with black stockings and high heels, and even more make-up than the few astonishing students I had seen about the school in the morning.

'G & T?' she asked, waving a long glass. 'Come through to the dining room and make yourself one. Or not.'

She walked in a cloud of perfume, a pungent and complex scent which would no doubt be devastating on a jiggle starlet, but seemed somehow decadent on the chairwoman of the English department. I expect that's unfair to my hostess – she was not on duty.

'Here,' she said, dropping some ice cubes into a glass. 'Fill it up. You can freshen mine while you're at it.'

'Thank you.'

'You like?' she asked, twirling to flounce out the skirt. 'It's a little number I got at Holt's. Your basic black dress.'

The spin was rather precarious, whether from the height of the heels or the gin I couldn't say.

'Enchanting!'

'You were looking rather doubtful,' with an edge of suspicion in her black eyes. 'You were probably thinking it would look better on a more petite woman.'

'Actually, I was reminded of Pamela Anderson.'

Ms Felsen stroked my cheek.

'That's about the sweetest thing anyone's ever said to me!'

Ms Felsen kissed my cheek.

'So what do you want to know?' She perched on a chair and crossed her legs, pulling her hem down toward her knee.

I opened the file on the table.

'If you could just explain ...'

She answered with more attention to detail than my officemate had, quickly clearing up my confusions about in-class and take-home work, attendance policy, plagiarism penalties, mid-term and final grading. But although her answers were practical, her mind was obviously elsewhere, and I found myself paying more attention to the woman than to her words.

Rather than talk eye to eye as women usually do, she kept glancing about the room, out the window, at her glass, at her legs. One hand played with her skirt hem, stroked her knee, her calf, her thigh, pulled the hem down again. From casual acquaintance – never having cohabited with a woman for more than six months or so, and they as jeans-clad as I – I have but scant knowledge of pantyhose, but Ms Felsen's looked expensive and luxurious; and she seemed entranced by the hard sheer sheen on her legs. Odd. While her right hand toyed with the glass, her left moved to her earring, her hair, her throat, stroking, fondling. But while her hand fluttered about her head, I noticed that her forearm was in fact pressing, caressing her breast.

As she talked about 'Ministerial Standards for Object-Oriented Learning for Fresh Start Students', Ms Felsen was making love to herself.

Or was she acting, in her imagination, as my proxy?

No, surely not.

'Enough of that nonsense,' she said. 'What do you think of the knick-knacks?'

Relieved, I looked about the room. Despite the warmth of the day, a fire blazed in the fireplace. Wood panelling, a large modern oil of a screaming woman, another of what purported to be a view into a flower but obviously was meant to be female and anatomical; a tall glass-doored cabinet with a collection of porcelain and pewter hedgehogs, tall windows with a view of the same wall I see from my windows (I'm just below that room); on the opposite wall shelves with dried flowers, a football with 'Fuddpuckers – Champions – 1963', a collection of decorative glass jars hand-labelled 'Flower Blossom Honey', 'Peach Mango Chutney', and 'Jalapeño Jelly'. In the place of honour on the mantelpiece stood hardcovers of *The Female Eunuch*, *Le deuxième sexe*, *The Feminine Mystique*, and other historic feminist texts, supported on either side by two bottles, each containing a reddish ovoid and labelled 'Thousand-Year Egg', a tribute perhaps to the millennium. Above, a large print of a family of hedgehogs in nineteenth-century English rural style. Visible beyond the front hall was the living room, which, from the glance I'd had, presented a similar collection – imaginative, eclectic, eccentric and touchingly personal, as if Ms Felsen were laying bare her deepest secrets, her most cherished memories.

'You like?'

'Very much. I was wondering how long I'd have to work at the college before I could afford a house like this one?'

'Forget it – I bought it for a song in the spring of '77, just after the PQ's first victory – now it's worth maybe thirty times what I paid for it. Otherwise, you like them?'

'Sorry ... uhh ...' I stammered, and for a confused moment wondered if she meant her thighs.

'My treasures.'

She held her hands up before her in a vaguely papal gesture.

Could she mean her breasts?

'My precious little treasures.'

Relief – neither thighs nor bosom could be described as *little*.

She spread her arms as if to embrace the fullness of the room.

'Nothing very expensive – well, a few, perhaps – but everything dear to me, everything humming with its own harmony of the past, my past ... history, aren't they, Tinker Bell?'

Hedgehogs? Chutney?

'Isn't Tinks just the cutest widdle doggie-woggie?'

She picked up the terrier and held it before her.

'Very cute.'

'I sometimes think she looks like wee Bernie Landry, the premier.'

She frowned and set the dog down.

'Thousand-year eggs suggest rather more past than ...'

'No, no, thousand-year eggs aren't really a thousand years old, I pickled them myself from a recipe in a Chinese cookbook.'

'And the football?'

'In high school I was a ... a cheerleader.'

'And the hedgehogs?'

'I adore hedgehogs. People confuse them with porcupines, because we don't have hedgehogs in North America, but porcupines are five, ten times the size of hedgehogs. Did you ever see hedgehogs when you were in ... where was it? Exeter?'

'Edinburgh. No, I saw no hedgehogs while I was there.'

They wouldn't last long round Tollcross or the Grassmarket.

'I haven't either and I try to get over every year or two ... not always Britain, mostly France these days, but ... oh, I'd love to see one ambling along a hedgerow, minding its own business. Really, I sometimes think the world would be a better place if we could all be hedgehogs ... all learn to mind our own business? ... Or? ...'

The doorbell interrupted her.

'Oh, goodness gracious me,' she cried, 'I've got to … Quiet, Tinker Bell …'

She pointed a remote control at the fireplace and the flames died.

'Sorry, Will … oh, where's my handbag?'

The chat had been turning decidedly treacly, and I was happy to depart.

But as I headed for the front door, Ms Felsen interposed her substantial if rather mincing presence between me and the vestibule.

'Will … ha-ha … I wonder if … relations with my sweetie lately, I expect you've heard the … not that you'd … I don't mean to … departmental gossip and all … but could you … well, I mean … would you be so kind as to use the inside basement stairs there and … I'm sorry I can't exp … Le cœur a ses raisons que la raison ne connaît point … ha-ha … must rush … I'm late, I'm late, for a very important date …'

I admit I was curious about her 'sweetie', but dared not follow Ms Felsen to the door; however, I delayed my descent to my proper quarters just long enough to catch a glimpse, by leaning a wee bit, of a long black limousine with tinted windows. A uniformed chauffeur held the door open, and as Ms Felsen bent to enter, I glimpsed a welcoming hand held out to her, and a pair of elegantly slim legs in sheer black stockings. Obviously the female partner of a second couple, or perhaps it was girls' night out. I finished my G&T and made my way down here.

Four

He minded little what tale was told since he had what he wanted.

antique volumes

September nearly over. I'm managing to stay a week or two ahead planning my in-class work, lectures, exercises, etc., while barely keeping up with the correcting. The office is a pleasant enough routine – I teach early, Harrison teaches through midday, and we have common office hours only on Tuesdays and Thursdays. Today, Thursday, when I returned from class, Harrison was slumbering in his chair.

'Resting my eyes, Ensign Ass, just resting my eyes as I composed a limerick.'

'I could see that,' I assured him. 'Anyone could have seen that.'

'You're lying again. You and anyone else would have concluded that I was grabbing a nap instead of imparting my wisdom to those few among the intellectually challenged students who are curious about the deeper realities – such as the great march of history from olden times, that is, the Era of the Spice Girls, down the long ages to modern times, that is, the Era of Britney Spears. Or whether France is a city in Paris or the other way about. Or how big was George Eliot's weenie.'

'I suppose in French class they want to know about George Sand's weenie.'

'That's the idea, young Franklyn, you're getting into the spirit of things.'

'If Bend It Spice and Posh Football are olden times, when's eternity?'

'October. Now, what do you know about Icelandic literature?'

'Uhh ... Sagas? Eddas?'

'Didn't you bump into any Icelanders on the Prairies? Aren't they pandemic out there?'

'Mostly in Manitoba, I believe. I met a few with Icelandic background, but they were mostly Canadianists like me. Oh, in Aarhus I met Gudrun, of course …'

'Ah, yes, the enchanting Ms Sigurdardóttir, Miss Lava Flow 1997. But *knowledge* – whether linguistic, historical or even, as I suspect it must have been, given Ms Sigurdardóttir's character, biblical – of one enigmatic Icelandic woman hardly amounts to a specialty in Icelandic language and literature?'

'I'm a wee bit busy with my courses just now.'

'Oh well, you've got till next August.'

'Beg pardon?'

'To swot up a specialty in Icelandic or Icelandic-Canadian literature. Best to learn some Icelandic, too. Helps when you order beer – Eitt bjor, gerðu swo vel.'

'But why would …'

'Because, Ensign Ass, after a winter in this madhouse you're going to need some relief. Next August there's a conference in Reykjavik of the Canada-Scandinavia Association. I'm going, and you might as well go with me.'

'I'm not sure I'll have enough money to …'

'Don't worry, I'll see that you get some money from the Faculty Conference and Book Fund. And you needn't actually deliver a paper, as long as the abstract looks scholarly.'

'I've never heard of the Canada-Scandinavia Association. Don't you mean the Nordic Association for Canadian Studies?'

'Good heavens, no – the NACS is a serious academic organization. The CSA is a modest but respectable operation run out of Oslo by a poet named Øystein. He sets up some lectures, but he concentrates on poetry readings – narcissist keening to narcissist across the lava fields – but frankly the CSA is better known for illegal smiles, liver damage and paternity suits …'

'Well …'

'Good. It's settled. I hope you have a strong suitcase for the duty free. You need a second mortgage to get wrecked in Reykjavik. Or perhaps you prefer fornication. How are you on blondes?'

'Same as brunettes, I guess.'

'*I love you for your mind, darling*. How sweet. The brunette Miss Hekla aside, Iceland is wall-to-wall in blondes. But it doesn't matter: booze or broads, we'll have a ball.'

'And you're an Icelandic scholar?'

'In a very small way. I have just enough Icelandic to construe *Egils saga Skallagrímsonar* with a crib, but not enough to get inside the poetry.'

'I'm afraid I...'

'*Egils Saga* in the vulgar tongue. Get yourself round to the library and borrow *The Collected Sagas of the Icelanders* in the handsome new five-volume set donated by the government of Iceland. Read at least *Egils Saga*, the fascinating biography of Egil Skallagrímsson, greatest of the skaldic poets. My hero. Along with Sir William Schwenk Gilbert, of course.'

'You're a poet yourself?'

'Guilty as charged.'

'I read most of the Canlit journals, but I don't recall seeing anything by ...'

'Oh, I don't write respectable stuff.'

'But ...'

'A wandering minstrel I – a thing of shreds and patches, of ballads, songs and snatches, but not much dreamy lullaby, though I do my bit for topsy-turvydom, the defining quality of Quebec. So, read *Egil's Saga* and buy a teach-yourself Icelandic – less than a year before the conference.'

'I'm really not sure ...'

'Nonsense, of course you're coming. Iceland isn't big enough for me and La Felsen, so we'll inevitably cross paths, if not swords, and you'll have to tag along to keep me mad ... order the drinks ... carry the bags ...'

'She's going too? Why all this flurry of interest in Icelandic literature?'

'Why, not? Medieval literature in the archaic tongue of a people who number just over a quarter of a million – a real grabber. But it is related to Old English. Ever do *The Seafarer*? *The Wanderer*?'

'Those, yes. I ... had a term of it ...'

'*The Dream of the Rood? Beowulf?*'

'Some *Beowulf*, yes.'

'Ah, the glories of the tongue:

> 'Hwæt, we Gar-Dena in geardagum
> Þeodcyninga þrym gefrunon,
> Hu þa æþelingas ellen fremedon!

'But I expect you have much of it by heart.'

'I'm afraid we studied it in translation.'

'In translation? Age of Lead! What debased coinage is fobbed off on us these days! What impoverished sensibilities! Are the folk of Montreal to entrust to you the education of little Stephanie and Tiffany, not to mention Gino, Vasilliki and Bok Choy? In translation? So you don't even know about thorn, eth, and ash?'

'*Thorn* is the name of the letter written as Þ capital and þ lowercase, and is the voiceless *th*. *Eth* is Ð or ð, the voiced *th*, and *ash* is the diphthong æ, a sort of *a*.'

'Exactly, letters used in Old English, and dropped by about Chaucer's time, but still used in Icelandic. But you need a bit more than recognizing a few exotic letters, and by the time we get to Keflavíkurflugvelli, you will. And much more.'

'Kefla ...?'

'Keflavik airport. Why am I having to explain this to a Doctor of Philosophy?'

'I'm not sure I ...'

'"O thou dull Moor! O gull! O dolt! As ignorant as dirt!" And is the airport dative or accusative, I wonder? In Latin – "And how's your Latin?" I ask disingenuously – it would be dative, but in Icelandic I think it's accusative.'

'I'm not sure I ...'

'Emilia? In *Othello*? It's a play? By Shakespeare?'

'Yes, I ...'

'Ye gods, did you hear that? I used a questioning tone for declaratives. I've been infected by the wretched students. I think I'd best blow my brains out; hand me your gun. No? A rope, then? A straight razor? Potassium cyanide? Though perhaps not – I have a class – that should be fatal.'

As I have become used to his tone, his abrupt dislocations, I find I enjoy, even delight in his conversation. The cracks about my ignorance were without malice, and were, I fear, deserved. Little Latin and less Greek, this Will as well.

'Harrison, are all the teachers here – I mean in the English department – as, well, as eccentric as you?'

'Me? Eccentric? I'm not eccentric, I'm starkers. And so are all the rest of them. Would you trust Ms Green Bay Packers there to tell you the time of day? Or mystical Miss Geysir? Or the Black Widow? And they're by no means the worst. The great one was never here, of course, but he knew us well:

> 'Things are seldom what they seem,
> Skim milk masquerades as cream;
> Highlows pass as patent leathers;
> Jackdaws strut in peacock's feathers.'

'W. S. Gilbert?'

'It sure isn't Egil Skallagrímsson.'

'Witty.'

'Witty? *Turbot is ambitious brill* – a profound comment on all things Québécois. And who is your hero?'

'I'm not sure I understand.'

'On whom did you lavish the last five or ten years of your precious young life? The subject of your doctorate.'

It was the inevitable question, and about which I am a mite sensitive. The answer is frequently a problem even on the Prairies, and because my subject was – or is, if as alleged he is still alive – obscure in other parts of Canada, the reaction is usually a blank look of embarrassed confusion. But Harrison was better informed than most.

'Augustus Smallweed? You did your doctorate on Augustus Smallweed, the Magus of Medicine Hat? Or was it Moose Jaw? The Caliph of Calgary, the Enigma of Edmonton, the Winnebago of Winnipeg?'

'Along with the Shaman of Saskatoon, the Wizard of Wascana, the Brahmin of Brandon, and so on. Smallweed was omnipresent.'

'Why Smallweed? Why not Wee-bee or Krotch or Kansellya or Van Oink or one of the other superstar cow-people?'

'Well, the Canlit trade is overpopulated. No matter how many writers there are out there, there aren't enough to fill the demand for dissertation subjects.'

'Scandalous.'

Harrison stood up.

'But enough of this scholarly profundity – I must to class. Just hand me my bullwhip, will you. And you'll be attending the departmental meeting at four?'

'I expect it might be politic. Will you be there?'

> 'To our prerogative we cling –
> So pardon us,
> So pardon us,
> If we decline to dance and sing,
> Tra la la …'

'More Gilbert and Sullivan?'

'Well spotted. Louis, this could be the beginning of a beautiful friendship. By the way, if you are going to the meeting, take along something exciting to read – Dr Taylor finds Henry James's *The Golden Bowl* is just the thing.'

'*The Golden Bowl* makes even *The Magic Mountain* look like a page-turner.'

'I prefer Hooker's *Ecclesiastical Polity*. And if you think they're boring, wait until you hear the stuff they're going to discuss at the meeting.'

'Can you at least tell me how to get to …' I tried to find the memo with the room and time.

Harrison groaned.

'You'll never find it on your own, Ensign Ass. All right, meet me here at ten to four and I'll show you the way, but only so far. I mustn't ruin my record.'

'Record?'

'I haven't been to a department meeting since 1981.'

Five

Most likely, the wearisomest, self-righteous Pharisee that ever ransacked a Bible to rake the promises to himself and fling the curses on his neighbours.

… took an opportunity of escaping into the free air.

'Let me give you some advice,' Harrison said as we entered the round tower, 'Keep your mouth shut – no questions, no comments – and vote Little Buttercup's line.'

'Just what I was planning to do.'

'And no matter how boring or bizarre it gets, do not gasp, sigh, groan, weep, tear your hair, or leap screaming from the roof waving genitals and manuscripts.'

'No leaps, no screams.'

'Beware hippos and toadies.'

'Hippos and toadies?'

'And don't buy anything.'

'What could …?'

'Sign nothing but the attendance sheet. Go up those stairs, and God help you.'

After the echoing gloom of the spiral stairs, the meeting room was bright from a ring of windows below a domed ceiling. The rose walls and dome gave the room a comforting warmth.

By the podium, Ms Felsen entertained a clutch of senior teachers. On one table stood a coffee machine flanked by mounds of muffins under plastic wrap. On another table lay several stacks of paper. A bald man was taking a sheet from each pile, so I did the same.

'You're new,' the bald man beamed. 'Eric Coombs – pleased to meet you.'

He grasped my hand.

'Will Franklyn.'

He grasped my arm.

'One word, Wilf – *retirement!*'

'I've only just …'

'It's never too early to think of your retirement – trust me, have I ever lied to you before?'

'Well, I …'

'One word – *outports!*'

'Outports?'

'A rustic retirement villa with – ta-dah! – an ocean view!'

'Possibly?'

'In a quaint, cosy outport! Wilf, I want you to do yourself a favour.' He tightened his grip on my arm and peered earnestly into my eyes. 'Look over this brochure, and next week I'll drop by and answer any questions you may have about this once-in-a-lifetime offer, can't ask more than that, eh, Wilfy-boy?'

He released my arm.

'You won't regret it, trust me.'

He patted my shoulder.

I glanced through the agenda and a group of reports on EW, WRE, ERW, and SLE – not only were the acronyms not explained, but many of the key words seemed to be in French, though of a vocabulary so recondite that my bookish fluency was useless.

Margaret Taylor slipped into the next chair. I had not seen her since that first day.

'Don't bother reading that,' she said. 'The ministry is mad. I'm Margaret Taylor in case you've forgotten.'

'I remembered the Margaret, and Harrison reminded me of the surname.'

'Is that all he told you?'

Eric's hand had left a sweaty print on my shirt.

'Well … substantially.'

'That's all right – he has nicknames for everyone. You're Ensign Ass and I'm the Black Widow or the Black Death. Sid over there is the Hound of the Basketballs, the woman in the flowery muu-muu is the Blancmange, the one with the greasy hair is the Wife of Bath, and she's talking to Sumo Surprise …'

'That bald guy, Eric something?'

'Eric the Red.'

'An Icelander?'

'Eric the red rantin' Tory out there in a dory, a-runnin' down Squires on the squid-jigging ground.'

I held up my brochure.

'One word – *retirement*!'

'One word – *outports*! Did he mention that those retirement villas, those outports, are in Newfoundland? It's his own retirement he's interested in. Meanwhile, we're marooned for the next thirty years on this island of broken dreams populated by creatures from a nightmare. I mean, look at them!'

The men had spread down and forward; their hair was white and thin. The women had spread sideways, and their hair, still in the styles of their youth, was miraculously untouched by grey. Most were dressed in memories of that bygone age of hippies, flower children, marches, sit-ins, sexual liberation and dope.

Margaret had been following my eyes.

'Harrison calls them the hippos.'

'Cruel but apt.'

'The junior ones are even worse – he calls them the toadies.'

She indicated half a dozen in their early thirties; they huddled together and gazed with awe toward Ms Felsen. Their earnest T-shirts protested global warming, globalization, illiteracy, poverty, the eating of whales, the eating of fish, the eating of meat. Both the males and the females seemed somehow sexless.

'The toadies come from the slums of university land.'

'Education degrees?'

'And we're in for a treat – Terpsichore Toadie is giving a presentation later.'

Ms Felsen cleared her throat.

'All right, people. People?'

In time they settled down, approved the minutes, the agenda.

'Now then,' said Ms Felsen, 'course descriptions. Cynthia has laboured long and hard' – a hand of approbation toward a beaming bulk spreading over a chair to Felsen's left – 'on the new model course description, and the ministry has decreed that it must be in use for next term. Now, this new model incorporates certain crucial changes, which Cynthia will, with her accustomed eloquence, outline for us. Cynthia?'

Cynthia Hippo heaved herself to her feet.

'Thank you, Madam Chair,' she cooed. 'Now, people, as we all know, object-oriented course structures have been in the works for eight years at least, but they have budded and flowered and been honed and primped and fine-tuned, and I must admit I am very excited about them, as I know you will be when you see what has been born of this mighty labour ...'

Margaret murmured close to my ear: 'When we see what rough beast slouches toward Bethlehem to be born ...'

'A clichéd beast obviously, a mixed metaphor beast.'

'Spawn of hippo.'

'I put my trust in great literature.'

'I put mine in Warren Buffett.'

I looked longingly at the stairs.

'How does one manage a surreptitious escape from a round room?' I whispered.

'Why would you want to? It's meant to be a womb.'

Among the handouts I found the paper Cynthia Hippo was talking about. It made no sense that I could see. When she launched into an enthusiastic justification of 'lancement intégrale de base' I turned to Margaret and rolled my eyes.

'I can guess what Harrison told you,' she hissed. 'You should have listened to him,' and turned over the book she was reading – *The Golden Bowl*.

In time Ms Felsen resumed the chair and we all voted to approve whatever it was that Cynthia Hippo had proposed.

'All right, people, the next item on the agenda is a delicate one. The executive has noted that several department members have not yet achieved proactive gender neutrality in their course descriptions, and as proactive gender neutrality is the stated policy of the department, and indeed of the ministry, we must all make every effort to achieve this end, especially where recent criticism has established grounds for such an approach. People, this is no longer a matter of individual discretion.'

She cocked her hand on her hip.

'Terminology. I must remind veterans and new faculty that the approved term is not *gay* but *queer*. So, people, let's all mind our p's and q's, and no puns intended.'

Widespread giggling as she consulted her paper.

'Now, American academics from Fiedler on have done wonders showcasing the essential queerness of American lit, and I know we are inspired by their lead. Proactive faculty have already privileged in their courses the queer subtexts in the works of such queer English authors as Shakespeare, Marlowe, the Brontës, George Eliot, E. M. Forster, Virginia Woolf and so on, but some of us continue to resist on some of the more contentious cases such as Wordsworth, Dickens, Orwell, Greene, Hughes and Heaney, and we're all going to have to make efforts in that direction. Now, those of you who want help in realigning your course materials can consult with Tabitha' – a hand of approbation toward a simpering hippo to Felsen's right – 'and her committee. I might add that they are currently focusing on Canlit, where they have already established the essential queerness in the work of such obvious figures as Isabella Valancy Crawford, Pauline Johnson, L. M. Montgomery, Findley, Van Herk, Atwood, Rule, Laurence and so on, and are at work on …? Tabitha …?'

Tabitha Hippo brought a sheet of paper from beneath her vast shawl and simpered, 'Well, among the Eastern Canadians we're tackling are Frank Scott, Munro, Richler, *Lay*ton' – a round of giggles – '*both* Cohens, Hood, Metcalf, Harris and Solway, and among the Westerners Bowering, Kinsella, Wiebe, Kroetsch, W. O. Mitchell, Smallweed and Kreisel.'

'Thank you, Tabitha and committee. I'm sure we're all very grateful, but we have much more to do, and anyone keen to form subcommittees for foreign authors in translation might check with me or with Tabitha so that we can begin work on the greats such as Flaubert, Zola, Tolstoy and Dostoevsky …'

I finally recovered from my stunned immobility.

'Margaret,' I whispered, 'is she trying to say that all those authors are gay?'

'Not gay, queer.'

'And now a special treat – Terpsichore is going to share with us an approach which she has found useful in her classes.'

'Her name really is Terpsichore?'

'Yes, hush.'

A scrawny drab in layers of mismatched clothes minced to the front. Her T-shirt proclaimed she would rather be naked than dressed in the skins of murdered animals; no one took her up on the offer.

'The secret!' she proclaimed, holding aloft a linen carry-all, 'is in the bag!'

She basked in the noisy appreciation of this witty sally.

'And what is the secret?'

She pulled a rounded piece of wood from the bag.

'Girls and boys, can we spell *Ouija board*?'

Margaret clutched my wrist. 'Don't,' she hissed, 'Don't move, don't say a word.'

'Can we spell *hush*?' I replied.

Terpsichore's argument for the Ouija board, revealed after ten minutes, was 'It gets them using letters!'

She retired in triumph.

After some announcements, Ms Felsen adjourned the meeting. I could sense an air of expectancy as she bent to the table then turned to hold up before her two gigantic cupcakes with pink frosting and a cherry in the middle of each. She paused for silence, then gave an exultant cry of 'Muffin time!'

With yips and grunts of delight, the department heaved itself to its feet and waddled toward the goodies, a lugubrious stampede from a TV documentary – feeding time in hippo heaven.

Margaret and I stood.

'I must admit,' I said, 'that this queer policy surprises me.'

'It shouldn't – you've been in grad school.'

'Yes, but I didn't realize things had reached such an insane level. Perhaps you'll explain it all to me sometime.'

She examined me with a cool eye.

'TGIF tomorrow?'

'Yes, sure, great.'

I wondered if I should tell Harrison about my date with Margaret, but he wasn't in the office, and I walked home, musing over my private hopes.

Six

Her bold, saucy look, and her ready words.

'Why canst thou not always be a good lass, Cathy?'
And she turned up her face to his, and laughed, and answered,
'Why cannot you always be a good man?'

'Libiamo,' said Margaret, and drank off half of her first martini.

'Libiamo?'

'Italian for *Let us drink*. From *La Traviata*.'

I was surprised to recognize the melody from the few bars she hummed.

'Then, Libiamo.'

Margaret had suggested happy hour at a place near the school. 'They also do light meals – sandwiches, salads, pastas – in case.'

Whatever she considered the object of the evening, I decided I'd best ask about school.

'How about you pull my teeth instead?'

'You promised.'

'Okay, for five minutes.'

'General advice?'

She pondered.

'Get the students focused correctly. They're good kids, but don't think university – you're not preparing them for a career in English studies. You're teaching a compulsory subject to kids who are going to be nurses, radiologists, teachers, accountants, draftsmen, engineers. Give them some good literature to read, help them enjoy it, understand it, write about it. The most important job you have is to teach them write clear prose so they can handle university and whatever writing their jobs might require.'

'Sounds sensible.'

'You'd be surprised. The hippos look to their pensions, and get

« 37 »

through the year repeating what they've been saying for thirty years about the Vietnam War, the heroism of Che Guevara, the wisdom of Herbert Marcuse. The toadies are earnest, but they've been trained to teach elementary school, so they underestimate the kids – for example, Twiggy Toadie does an entire course in which the kids illustrate rap music with magic markers.'

'Okay, no rap, no magic markers. But the lunacy at the meeting yesterday – does Ms Felsen believe all that stuff?'

'Of course not. Heidi is a great head of department because she knows that what teachers really care about is their schedules. You have some lousy eight o'clocks because you were hired at the last minute, but by next year she'll get you what you want. Beyond that, she acts as a barrier between the teachers and the administration and the ministry. See, you can always depend on the Quebec government being in the van of the latest progressive ideas – of twenty years ago. Such as queer lit. You can hardly be surprised – surely you've encountered the new orthodoxies?'

She sat erect, her hands moving decisively, her diction crisp. She was remarkably attractive.

'Oh yes, gender studies are big at the U of A, but that stuff yesterday is gender studies with the brains kicked out. I expect I can learn it, but can I learn to live with it?'

'Learning to live with it is not enough – *He loved Big Brother.* In Quebec, the government knows what's best for you. In Quebec, mass movements, democratic movements, are initiated from the top.'

'That's not democracy, it's autocracy, aristocracy, bureaucracy, paternalism.'

'The Bourbon lilies weren't emblems of liberté, égalité, fraternité.'

She began on her second martini.

'Look, haven't you done any deconstruction?' she asked. 'Pursuit of the opposite sex implies its reverse, pursuit of the same sex.'

'But how can they argue that Layton and Cohen, the most priapic poets in Canadian literature, are gay?'

'The more women Irving shtupped, the more queer he must have been.'

'But Frank Scott wasn't promiscuous, never mind queer. And Alice Munro? Rudy Wiebe?'

'Repressed promiscuous, therefore repressed queer.'

'Out west, folk say W. O. Mitchell and his wife had the happiest marriage in recorded history.'

'Then they'll find a photo of his wife wearing slacks. Or perhaps discovering voyeurism in his work: *Who has seen the window?*'

'If it weren't so sad it would be hilarious.'

'Wait till the ethnic committee reports.'

'Why am I not surprised?'

'Together, those two committees will want you to find at least one new queer writer and one writer of colour to include in every course. Find a queer writer of colour and you're a star.'

'Wole Soyinka? Chinua Achebe?'

'No, they're black, but no one in the department would have the balls to call them queer, at least not while they're alive. Of course, the ministry doesn't care because they write in English, so they're irrelevant. No, what you want is a one-armed black lesbian single mother translated from impenetrable French.'

'Vivian Richards?'

'I expect she'll do, whoever she is.'

'A West Indian cricket superstar in the eighties.'

'Well, he must have a ghost-written autobiography, so use that – they'll never have heard of cricket, and will certainly never have heard of him. Of course, the orthodoxy is that all jocks are automatically queer – all that assertive masculinity. They'll fall all over themselves thanking you for finding such a multi-threat addition to the list of recommended writers.'

'I'm surprised the authorities don't want to add a separatist component.'

'They do, and of course there is no dearth of queer Québécois writers, but not a one of the vieille souche is black, black not being prominent in the Norman and Breton gene pools.'

'But how can I stand in a classroom teaching these lies to the students?'

'Classroom? Students? You have missed the point that Heidi understands so well – this has nothing to do with classrooms and students. The ministry is obsessed with course descriptions. With politically correct course descriptions in hand, fonctionnaires who earn twice your salary can jet off to educational conferences of La Francophonie in Niger or the Ivory Coast waving your course descriptions to prove how progressive they are. Meanwhile, you're back here actually teaching testosterone junkies like Hemingway or Layton.'

As the tone got sillier, Margaret no longer sat erect, but leaned her elbows on the bar, flourished her hands vaguely, and toyed with her martini. I suggested we might eat. It looked like being a very long evening, or a very short one.

A basket of garlic bread arrived with the menus and I was relieved when Margaret ate a few slices. Through the hearty soup and a pasta she drank the wine with enthusiasm but not excess, and gradually regained some precision in her gestures and speech.

'Last question, Margaret. I suppose this is terribly haughty of me, but the department obviously prefers to hire toadies; what are we doing here?'

'You have to understand the psychology of hiring committees. If you had the task, who would you hire?'

'The best qualified, the most accomplished, the most capable – it's obvious, surely?'

'For you, yes – accomplished people hire the most accomplished applicants they can find, even applicants smarter than themselves. Stupid people feel threatened by intelligence so they hire people stupider than themselves. Thus the hippos hire toadies. But the committee can't meet during the summer and winter vacations, and Heidi controls last-minute hiring. Harrison got her to hire me. And you?'

I told her about meeting Gudrun at the Aarhus conference.

'Ah, the explosive Ms Eruption.'

'A new name for her.'

'I can think of a number of others, but they're not for polite company.'

'You're not a fan?'

She swirled the wine gently, took a thoughtful sip.

'I admit she's an accomplished scholar and a capable prof – Harrison also recommended her – but I'm not convinced by her flakiness alternating with the soi-disant profundity of soul – *I am an Icelandic seeress!* That Icelandic word that sounds like *vulva*. Apt. One of these days I'm going to investigate any Gudruns in the sagas.'

'Well, her prediction about the job worked out for me. I'm grateful for that.'

Margaret regarded me coolly.

'It's none of my business, of course, but if I were you I'd be cautious – Gudrun eats men.'

True, but not perhaps as Margaret meant it.

I was relieved when she bent to her food, a signal that the subject was closed. 'So what do you think of your officemate?'

She was studying a piece of cuttlefish on her fork.

'He's certainly interesting. I never know what he's going to say next.'

'I expect you're acquainted with his reputation.'

'Yes, I gather he has published several books of poetry. I've glanced through his bookcase, but couldn't ...'

'I meant his reputation with women.'

'I'd heard something of it, but these things are often exaggerated.'

'Possibly, but Harrison is undeniably a very charming, sexy man.' At last she looked me in the eye. 'Irresistible to some women.'

I paused.

'Margaret, I've never been much of a diplomat, but I think perhaps this is none of my business.'

'Diplomatically put. But I want to explain. In my final term at the college, I took a course from Harrison. The attraction was mutual, but he never gets mixed up with students. Later, while I was at McGill, we got together, but then I went away for my post grad. Since I've returned we've been friends – it is a warm and affectionate friendship, but nothing more.'

'Margaret, you needn't have ...'

'Have I made myself clear?'

'Yes, but ...'

'But me no buts. A nightcap in the bar? Cognac? Or do you prefer armagnac? calvados?'

'I'm afraid that ten years of TA pay have precluded such rich drinks.'

'You can afford them now. And an espresso.'

'Always a treat – I'm used to instant.'

Margaret sighed.

The sobriety she had regained during the meal evaporated in the fumes of cognac. In twenty minutes she was finished and suggested we walk the two short blocks to her apartment.

'I rather think I'll hold your arm,' she said.

'My pleasure.'

When we got to the building, she asked if I would like a coffee.

'Thanks, Margaret, but perhaps not tonight.'

'I mean ... I mean I live on the top floor and there's no elevator. I think perhaps I could use some help with the stairs.'

In the vestibule, she gave me her keys and asked me to get her mail from the box.

'And which is the key for the inside door?'

In time, with slips, stumbles, giggles, shushes, I got her inside her apartment and groped for a light. Would it be, I wondered, as neat and fastidious as the daytime Margaret, or as dishevelled as the evening one?

Neat and fastidious. Angular furniture with steel and black leather, three steel-framed abstracts, modular bookcases with all the volumes carefully arranged. No flowers, no vases for flowers – austere and utilitarian.

I would have preferred to help her to the couch and escape, but she muttered, 'Bedroom,' and leaned toward the door to the left. I helped her through and, as decorously as I could, onto the bed. I was turning to look for a blanket when she grasped my neck and pulled my head down for a fierce kiss. When my back began to hurt, I knelt by the bed, and saw that her skirt was up about her thighs. As she turned toward me, the hem rose higher. I tugged it back toward her knees.

'Would you like me to make you a coffee?'

'Not coffee, take my clothes off.'

She reached for the buttons of her blouse, but I held her hands.

'No, Margaret,' I murmured, 'not now, not like this.'

She struggled briefly, then lay back and closed her eyes.

'No ... I meant ... no, you're right ...'

She gave a brief laugh, but a tear broke from her eye and drew a line of make-up down her temple. I pulled a tissue from the box on the night table and dabbed at it.

'Then take off my clothes so I can sleep ... don't want to wake up with my clothes on.'

'I'm not sure ... can't you manage yourself?'

'Take them off ... it doesn't matter ... no false modesty.'

What now?

I got the covers out from under her, removed everything but bra and panties, and pulled the covers over her. By the time I had her blouse and skirt draped on a chair, she was gently snoring. I turned off the lights, locked myself out, and slipped the key under the door.

As I started the walk for home, I couldn't help reflecting that Margaret's moods suggested tensions I'd be wise to avoid.

Seven

Her spirits were always at high-water mark, her tongue always going – singing, laughing, and plaguing everybody who would not do the same. A wild, wick slip she was – but she had the bonniest eye, and sweetest smile, and lightest foot in the parish; and, after all, I believe she meant no harm.

Eric the Red rolled into the office.

'Wilf? One word – *retirement!* Remember me? Eric Coombs?'

'I'm sorry, Eric, but ...'

'Fact – the good Lord isn't making any more ocean frontage, Wilf, that's one of the hard truths of the real estate business.'

'I'm really not ...'

'Fact – every bay and cove in Newfoundland is dotted with picturesque outports, am I right or am I right? Fact – for years the government has been moving people away from the outports. Fact – hundreds of quaint yet historic houses are just sitting there empty and no one to enjoy – ta-dah! – that superb ocean view!'

Harrison strode in.

'Out!' he said.

'Gimme a break, Harrison, I'm just ...'

'Ensign Ass does not want to buy a derelict shack ...'

'Charming villa!'

'... on your windswept rock.'

'Bracing sea breezes!'

'Begone!'

Eric went.

'And he's not the only scam artist – Eric peddles stuff, others peddle franchises. On guard, Ensign Ass – this office is off limits to the lot of them.'

I saluted.

'Other than Eric the Red, how was the meeting?'

« 45 »

'Insane and confusing.'

'Then you need someone to explain things to you.'

'Actually, someone did.'

'You're coyness betrays you – my guess is Dr Margaret Taylor abraded the shine off the ministry and charmed the pants off you.'

'No,' I replied coolly, 'we went for drinks and pasta, we walked to her apartment, I dropped her off, then walked home.'

'No hanky-panky?'

'No hanky-panky.'

'Hmm …'

A few days later Margaret stopped me in the hall.

'Thank you for your discretion with Harrison,' she murmured.

'I wasn't being discreet – we walked to your place, said good night, and I walked home.'

'And that's all?'

'That's my story and I'm sticking to it.'

'You're very sweet, Will. And I'm usually more careful with booze on dates. I thought just for once I could relax a bit.'

'Martinis sneak up on one, I hear.'

'They do. We must get together again sometime.'

'Yes, let's.'

She paused.

'Not this weekend – I'm seeing my friend Julia – we went to McGill together – and then I have stacks of corrections to do.'

'Likewise. Give me a shout when you're free.'

That was before Thanksgiving, nearly two weeks ago, and no shout yet. A good thing I haven't been holding my breath – and no plans to do so.

When I checked my e-mail on the Friday morning before Hallowe'en, I found the daily posting from the Smallweed chat group; an announcement from Jeremy Toadie of a 'Lunchtime Slam Session! Finding the Pedagogical Role Model for the Milennium! Emily Brontë vs. Buffy the Vampire Slayer!'; and a letter from hekladottir@postnet.dk in the hasty typing which seems characteristic of everyone's e-mail:

will/ ill be in mtl for flying weekend visit, some stuff to clear up, what a mess, and sure you won't mind if i stay with you, ill be arivving midaft fri, dont meet me at dorval, ill get to your place on my own, after all, used to live there, lock up your glassware ha-ha, rushing/ play it again sam, 　　Gudrun

She hadn't specified which Friday, but the e-mail was dated the day before – she could be here in a few hours, so I would have to come straight home from class. If her visit had anything of the mood of our time in Aarhus, it might be enjoyable to play it again.

I went to Aarhus (or Århus as the Danes have it) last April after seeing the call-for-papers announcement in the English department office in the unlovely David Hume Building of Edinburgh University. The theme of the conference was 'Wrinkles in a Flat Landscape: The Prairie Enigma'. Nothing from the Prairies is more enigmatic than Smallweed, so I scrounged the fare and went over to deliver a paper. It was well enough received – finish a bit short of your allotted fifteen or twenty minutes, and you'll always be loved – and sat to listen to the next paper.

Gudrun made her way to the podium in a chaos of falling papers, pens, sunglasses, combs, giggles and apologies. After shuffling through her papers with more giggles and apologies, after arranging and rearranging her pens, talking a sip of water, she pushed her hair back, reset the combs, giggled, and announced:

'The title of my paper is "The Gift of Sight: Women in the Novels of Svandis Svavarsdóttir." The point is ... where is ... oh, here, yes, anyway, the paper is about how the women in Svandis's novels were the real powers of the Manitoba immigrant settlements, because every one of her heroines is a skörungur – that's Icelandic for an independent woman, a woman of strong character – they're known for their will power, their determination, their solidarity, and they are so adept, so adroit ...'

When she spilled the water on her skirt, Gudrun joined in the riot of laughter with as much enthusiasm as the others.

'More importantly, in several of her novels, her heroine is a völva, a seeress with the gift for prophecy, and this a gift is common among Icelandic women ...'

I doubt anyone listened to her rambling account of matriarchal supremacy in the dreary, ponderous tomes of Ms Svavarsdóttir. Gudrun was five minutes past her time limit when she said, 'Having finished the introduction, I now move on to the main body of my argument, which is that ... What? Really? Surely not, I mean ... Oh, it *is*, yes, well, Professor Carlsen, time *always* seems to be slipping away faster than ... don't you find ... oh, well, critics say the first page of a novel should contain the whole, so my introduction will have to stand for the whole. So, without further ado, I'll thank you, and ...'

As she stepped away from the podium, she knocked the water carafe flying, then dropped her papers and pen. As she bent to retrieve the paper, the seam of her skirt parted, revealing her winsome buttocks, bare but for the thin strand of a black thong panty. I spent the afternoon wandering about Aarhus. Stepping out of the Domkirke, I decided I needed a beer and a cheap meal. The square in front offered stainless steel fast food and banking, but in the narrow street along the side of the cathedral a bar-restaurant named Casablanca looked appealing. I was scanning the menu on the doorpost when I became aware of frantic waving through the window reflection. What now? Then I recognized Gudrun beckoning me in.

'Hi, you were just before me and my disaster, weren't you. You were a proper scholar, but you have to admit they'll remember my bottom longer than they'll remember your paper on ...'

'Smallweed?'

'Smallweed, yes, he's a crashing bore, but then so is Svandis Svavarsdóttir. But I'm not a bore, and I was sitting here all alone feeling sorry for myself when I saw you coming along, and I thought maybe you wouldn't be a bore either, even though you are a Canadian.'

She rearranged the combs in a futile effort to tame her flyaway brown hair.

'I thought all Icelandic women were blonde?'

'Lots are, but it's a funny thing about the Scandinavian blonde gene – look around you.'

I scanned the room.

'It descends to the women, not the men,' I concluded.

'Same in Iceland. And what do you suppose pays the rent in Scandinavian drugstores?'

'Miss Clairol? L'Oréal?'

'Got it in one.'

'So despite the accent you're not Canadian?'

'Well, I've lived there since I was seven, but I've kept my Icelandic citizenship.'

'And your Icelandic name – Gudrun Sigurdardóttir?'

'Very good. But in Icelandic Gudrun is with an *eth*, G-u-ð-r-u-n, and we put a *v* sound after the *G* – Guðrún.'

'Gvuthroon?'

'Close.'

'I think I'll stick to Gudrun.'

'Even the Danes do.'

'And are you … what was the word? A strong woman.'

'Skörungur – a woman of strong character. Obviously. And although people think I'm a flake, I'm also a völva …'

A wave of her hand swept her glass to a shattered end; the mineral water doused the skirt of the woman at the next table. The victim listened to Gudrun's flurried apologies with a whimsical smile, then in elegantly accented English said, 'But, my dear, I came to Casablanca for the waters.'

We ordered pasta and traded stories. Gudrun's father had shipped frozen seafood for Icelandair cargo, but accepted a job with, I gather, Eastern Provincial Airlines, which merged with Canadian, which merged with Air Canada. They had lived 'all over Leifur Eiríksson's Vinland' – in Newfoundland, on the Quebec North Shore, then Rimouski, then New Brunswick, then … but she was as vague about her geography as are the sagas, and the story tumbled out with such scattered rapidity that I was unable to keep the details straight. Gudrun attended a hodge-podge of schools and universities, and with her doctoral courses at McGill out of the way, got hired by Ms Felsen. Now she was on leave to finish her thesis research in Aarhus.

With her wilful hair, sharply etched lips, scanty make-up, and eccentric clothes, she was not conventionally beautiful. But her trim and peculiarly erect figure, merry chocolate-brown eyes, and good cheer made her increasingly attractive. Although she was one of those who must touch as they talk, she gave off no hint of flirtation that I could sense, so I readily gave myself over to the delights of companionship with no expectation of further adventures.

After dinner and a few more drinks, Gudrun said she had to get to bed, so we called for our bills.

'Oh, crumbs,' she exclaimed as she rummaged in her purse, 'I must have left my wallet at home. I can't even get money from the cash machine … oh, here, I have … take them, I'm really sorry, I really am a flake …'

She thrust some Danish coins and bills into my hand and stood up, inevitably knocking over her chair, dropping her scarf, and hitting a man on the head with her shoulder bag. Outside we headed uphill toward the university; I had to correct her navigation only twice.

'I've just been in Aarhus a little while,' she protested. 'Well, six months or so … well, okay, I have a lousy sense of direction … but I have a great *feel* for the place … did you see the cute pig statues in front of City Hall?'

I had a room in visitors' quarters on the top floor of some sort of science building; Gudrun had a bachelor flat fitted into a small house on a street running beside the campus.

'Well, good night, Gudrun. It's been …'

'I said I have to get to bed, not to sleep – aren't you coming in?'

'Well, I …'

'I have to warn you that Icelandic seeresses have greater powers if they're virgins, but I'm sure we can think of other ways to amuse ourselves …'

We did.

And now Gudrun was coming to visit.

Or something.

I assumed Gudrun would splurge on a cab from the airport or bus station then borrow the money to pay for it, but I underestimated her resourcefulness, for she arrived in a private car just as I was getting back from work.

'… and thanks very much, kiss-kiss, it's been very nice meeting you …'

The driver was young, handsome and well dressed. When Gudrun bent to wave goodbye, a card fluttered to the ground.

'You've lost something.'

'Oh, it's just his stupid business card. I expect he thinks he can get me into bed in return for the ride, but I've got to keep my powers pure and strong.'

We hugged and I carried her bag inside.

I have essays to correct, I wanted to caution her, but what was the point? And am I so locked into my job already? Am I such a spoilsport? In any case, she was staying only two nights, then going on to Toronto.

'I stopped in Montreal to see you,' she said with a winsome smile, 'and because it was cheaper.'

I doubted it was cheaper, but wondered why she would want to see me.

'And to see the boss about something to do with your job?'

I pointed toward the ceiling.

'That too.'

'And what would you like to do while you're here? I mean, besides chatting with Ms Felsen?'

'Ms Felsen? … Oh, yes, of course. Well, I'll see her tomorrow. But what about tonight? Have you found anything like the Casablanca?'

'I'm sure you know Montreal better than I do.'

'Let's talk about it on the way. But what time is it?'

'Just coming on five.'

'Too early to go out. What does one do in Montreal for cinq-à-sept?'

'Well …'

With a flourish of enthusiasm she sent her coffee cup flying.

❦

Eight

Eating and drinking, and singing and laughing, and burning their eyes out before the fire.

Screaming at the farther end of the room, shrieking as if witches were running red hot needles into her.

Put him in the cellar.

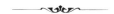

As far I can tell, our encounter with Harrison was entirely accidental. We filled up on couscous in one place, had a few drinks in a second, a few more in a third, and met him in a cosy little place on Drummond or Stanley.

'Great Thor, it's Miss Geothermal Energy herself. When did you blow into town? And how many others survived the crash?'

'Beast!'

'Satisfactory flight, I trust?'

'Flights – Copenhagen to Frankfurt to Montreal, and I hardly slept a wink, my dreams kept waking me up, and I'm glad we ran into you, you can tell me what they mean – they're about Will.'

'Ensign Ass as Dream-boy? Unlikely.'

'No, listen, Harrison, be serious, this is important.'

'I thought *you* were the Volvo, pudenda, whatever.'

'Völva, and don't be crude. Anyway, when it's one of my own dreams I like a second opinion. In the first dream Will was in a crowded disco and he was wearing a strange winged helmet, antique bronze it was, but somehow the helmet got knocked off and he lost it.'

'I wonder who did that?'

'Listen! Anyway, he lost the first hat, but it didn't bother him, and he kept on dancing and I woke up because we were landing in

« 53 »

Frankfurt. Then, after we took off again, in the next dream he was climbing a round white mountain, Vatnajökull, perhaps, but it had two peaks so maybe it's Mount Royal, and he was wearing this gigantic, flamboyant black hat with a scarlet band and a wide brim and gold rings, and it had a gigantic peacock feather, but the feather kept getting in his eyes, so he hung the hat on a little stump and he kept climbing.'

'A mountain of essays, obviously, ready to erupt when the students complain that he demands they be literate.'

'And in the third dream, he was lost in a stainless steel maze ...'

'Frankfurt airport obviously.'

'... and he didn't have a hat, but he caught a glimpse of a hat, it was black with silver trim, and he chased after it, but every time he came to a corner, the hat disappeared around the next corner, and he just knew it was the perfect hat for him, and he kept chasing it and chasing it through the steel maze, and then I woke up because they announced we were flying over Nova Scotia and that's how I knew for sure it was Will, and the dreams mean something important.'

'The third hat is obviously his search for the impossible – a literate student, a pay raise, one solid fact about the wretched Smallweed ...'

Gudrun punched him and turned to me.

'... or the end of Quebec referenda.'

'He's impossible, but if he knew about Guðrún Ósvífursdóttir in the *Laxdæla Saga* he'd take my dreams seriously, because they're prophetic.'

'Perhaps I don't want to know my future.'

'My future,' said Harrison, 'involves another Scotch – Krystal! And give these two something to keep their mouths occupied.'

As she prattled to Harrison, Gudrun as usual punctuated her remarks with touches, taps and strokes, but I noticed that from the first her leg was against Harrison's; soon enough she had her other leg between his. Though he regarded her with his characteristic disdain, he did not rebuff her.

'It's not my fault, things just happen,' she protested, knocking over her a stack of beer mats. Harrison asked her if she had managed to destroy Aarhus yet.

'They don't have earthquakes in Denmark, silly.'

'And have you managed to corrupt their English department?'

'That's unworthy of you, you know I never ...'

'What, never?'

'No, never!'

'What, *never*?'

'Well, hardly ever!'

'You know your *Pinafore*, but can you keep it on? Krystal!'

After two or three more drinks, Gudrun mentioned jet lag, and I admitted I was ready to leave too.

'I'll drive you,' said Harrison.

As he had clearly been massaging the mahogany for some hours, I suggested we share a cab.

'Ensign Ass, don't be an ass – this is Quebec: not even the cops can pass a breathalyser.'

'But ...'

He waved off my objection.

'Krystal!' and, circling his finger at us, handed the barmaid his credit card.

'You don't have to pay for me,' I objected.

'Thank you, Harrison,' said Gudrun, and stroked his thigh.

'Unhand me, woman, and get your coat on. Or off?'

The house was a blaze of lights, and people moved about in the living room.

'Princess Ida is obviously having a party, so let's crash it.'

Gudrun grabbed his arm with both hands and declared, 'Suddenly my jet lag is gone!'

I pointed out that while Harrison has tenure, neither Gudrun nor I do.

'Good point, Ensign Ass, but I'm the enterprising burglar who loves to hear the little brook a-gurgling. Wait down the steps.'

When the door opened, Gudrun gasped and covered her mouth to stifle her surprise when our chairlady appeared in a red satin and black lace bustier, flouncy black miniskirt, black hose, red high heels and a matching mask over her eyes.

'Harrison, you great lout, what are you doing here?'

'With a shake of his poor little head he replied,
"Oh, willow, titwillow, titwillow"!'

'Well, piss off, Titwillow, or I'll sic Tinker Bell on you – Tink, don't let him in!'

The ball of fur came yipping along the hall.

'So please you, ma'am, we much regret if we have failed in etiquette … And look who's blown into town – the Scourge of the Seacoasts, Ms Acksy Dent … though not prone at the moment.'

'Gudrun?'

Ms Felsen peered down at us.

'Sweetie!' she cried, tripping precariously down the steps. 'When did you arrive? Why didn't you call me? Where are you staying? Come in, come in! Why aren't you in Sweden?'

'Denmark, Hei … Heidi.'

Gudrun seemed oddly flustered.

'Denmark, Sweden, who cares, darling? Come on in. Drinkies?' waving her G & T.

'Golly, sure.'

They helped one another up the steps and past Harrison.

'What about us?'

'I told you, Harrison, piss off. Tinker Bell – kill!'

'Lighten up, Buttercup. After all, I brought you the ambulatory accident.'

'Oh, all right. But I warn you, it's a Hallowe'en costume party, and you'll feel out of place.'

'I'm coming as myself, the most cunning disguise of all.'

'It's a special sort of Hallowe'en costume party.'

What now?

'As long as there's booze and broads. By the way, Heidi, what are you supposed to be?'

'The Merry Widow.'

'Call me Frou-Frou in drag, and this lanky babe is Jou-Jou dressed as Ensign Ass.'

I am slow about these things, but even I soon got the point. When I thought about it, I realized that although Heidi is obviously a very sexual woman, she has never actually flirted with me, and I have never seen a man about the place, so what *special sort* meant came as no great surprise.

The guests had taken great pains over their costumes. Some were feminine, such as Marie Antoinette, Carmen, Judy Garland, Marilyn Monroe, Evita Peron and Mary Tudor with *Calais* stitched over her heart. Among the masculine were the Duke of Wellington, John Wayne, Groucho Marx and General Patton. Then there were the rather ambiguous Joan of Arc, Brünnhilde, and Boadicea in their metal bras, Marlene Dietrich in white tie and tails, and Queen Christina of Sweden, or perhaps Greta Garbo playing Queen Christina.

I did feel out of place.

But Gudrun and Harrison obviously did not – she was having a tactile chat with Ms Felsen, while Harrison plucked a pear from a fruit bowl on the hall table and stuffed it in his breast pocket.

'I'm an Amazon,' he declared. 'I trust that puts me in the spirit of things. Should I go the rest of the way? A bit of surgical intervention? Is there a doctor in the house?'

An Indian princess touched her tomahawk to his groin.

'Careful, babe, I know of at least three doctors in the house.'

'In that case, I think I'll have a drink. A double.'

'I'll get it,' said Gudrun. 'Come and help me, Will.'

We made our way through a stream of guests including a gladiator, a mermaid, and Liza Minnelli in *Cabaret* garb.

'I thought it was gay guys who went in for this sort of thing,' Gudrun whispered, 'dressing up and all, and lesbians looked like princesses or truck drivers. They must have spent a fortune on their costumes. What did Harrison want a double of?'

'Women.'

'He's come to the wrong place for that.'

He'd been drinking Scotch at the bar, so I poured him a double, a vermouth for Gudrun and the same for me.

'Here you go,' I said. 'Heidi's got great taste in interior decoration, hasn't she?'

'Super, yeah. Oh look, thousand-year eggs – they're new. I mean new here, not … Anyway, imagine, something almost as old as the Icelandic parliament.'

'Actually, she told me she pickled them from a recipe in a Chinese cookbook. Vinegar and soy sauce I suppose. I'll take Harrison his drink.'

As I handed him his glass, he was ogling Cleopatra. 'Great asp,' he remarked. She lashed him with her rubber snake.

A petite Ilse She-Wolf of the SS pressed her studded leather bosom against my arm, stroked my crotch with her swagger stick, and murmured something in a thick accent.

'I'm sorry, I don't understand French very well.'

She spat out something equally impenetrable and strode off, patting the behind of the Bride of Dracula as she passed.

'What did she say, Harrison?'

'*Oh, willow, titwillow, titwillow.*'

'No, tell me – I live in Quebec now, I should be able to understand.'

'Rendered in a mid-Atlantic accent she first said, "Comme tu es butch, ma chérie," and when she realized the truth she said, "Cawliss, un ostie d'bloke, pis une maudite tête-carrée." Though I'd be surprised if she got her genders straight – as you can see, they rarely do in Quebec.'

'I'll never be able to understand Montreal French.'

'Imagine them trying to understand Newfie or Bronx or Strine.'

I decided to finish my drink and leave. I was trying not to watch Miss Jean Brodie exploring Helen of Troy's intimate parts when I remembered that Gudrun didn't have a key to my flat. Of course, given her whimsy, and what she'd been up to in the bar, she might be sleeping at Harrison's. I decided to tell her I would leave the interior door unlocked and trust that she could manage to get in without waking me.

She was in the dining room with her arm around Heidi; I murmured the instructions, and was making my way back to the hall, when Tinker Bell went frantic; Ilse was attacking Gudrun with her swagger stick. Gudrun, no slouch, replied by decorating Ilse's front with a quiche. Ms Felsen showed her leadership by grabbing both combatants by the hair and holding them apart. She had help from the Sugar Plum Fairy, Wonder Woman and Theda Bara in her serpentine bra.

EIGHT

I passed Harrison in the doorway.

'Amazons at war?' he asked.

'A brief misunderstanding, I believe.'

> 'Schoolgirls we, eighteen and under,
> From scholastic trammels free,
> And we wonder – how we wonder! –
> What on earth the world can be!'

I lay in bed pondering the sexual preferences of my friends in Montreal – the promiscuous waif who sent me here is a virgin, my ageing officemate is a stud, my only romantic interest is a possibly alcoholic ice princess, and my voluptuous landlady, who seemed to be coming on to me, is a lesbian. Harrison says things in Quebec are never what they seem. Well, I've only been here two months, and I'd gone past the *seem* to the *are* with these four.

But now, as I write these notes on Saturday afternoon, I know I had more to learn about one of them.

Nine

Why, Cathy, you are quite a beauty! I should scarcely have known you – you look like a lady now.

My musings, the music and the murmurs kept me awake no more than five minutes, and I was enjoying a second coffee with the newspaper when Gudrun entered, frazzled, babbling.

'Oh, Will, I'm sorry, I didn't want to wake you, and I guess I didn't, but I hope you aren't angry at me ...'

'That's all right – I've been up for over an hour.'

'Well, that too, but I'm sorry about not sleeping here, but ...'

'I understand you have lots of friends in Montreal.'

'Yes, but ... ohh, it's so complicated. I mean, first I had to stay with you, because Harrison can't be bothered with e-mail, so I had to e-mail you, but I've been wild about Harrison for ages, and he can't be bothered with me, and then there's Heidi, and that was really complicated for me, I mean our thing was finished a couple of years ago, she was beginning it before I left last year, her ...'

'Slow down until I get your coffee, and what was finished and what was beginning?'

'Us, our thing was finished. Well, it was only for a little while, just after I started part-time. It was the operations that were beginning ... well, of course, he'd already started with the hormone treatments, and ...'

What now?

'He? Hormone treatments?'

'Oh crumbs, you mean you didn't know? I was sure Harrison must have ... I seem to have done it again, haven't I?'

'You might as well tell me everything.'

'Well, perhaps not everything,' with a coy smile. 'Anyway, Heidi used to be Hymie, and I had a little fling with Hymie while he was still a man. And not long after that he and his wife split up, it had

« 61 »

nothing to do with me, I swear it didn't, they split up because Hymie decided he'd rather be a woman. And I thought you knew because he never really made a secret about becoming Heidi. I mean, he was in the department for over twenty years as a guy, so people were obviously going to notice if he came to work in high heels, a skirt, and lip gloss. Though during the hormone treatments he was mostly dressed in slacks and loose sweaters, so you often didn't notice the changes happening, his breasts and his hips and all. And he was still Hymie even though everyone knew, at least everyone in the department, I don't think the students guessed. Then as soon as the term was over last spring, he had the operation, and that's when he changed his name and started wearing women's clothes, but just before that I left for Denmark, so last night was the first time I saw him, saw her as a woman.'

'It's ironic – when I met Heidi, I thought she was heterosexual, because once or twice it seemed to me she was perhaps flirting with me. Then when we got to the party and everyone seemed to be lesbian, I assumed Heidi was lesbian. And now you're telling me a man named Hymie became a woman named Heidi so he could become a lesbian?'

'Of course.'

'And was he a gay man? No, you said he was married.'

'No, he sure wasn't gay. Just the opposite. Hymie loved women, he couldn't keep his hands off them, he was way worse than Harrison, Hymie did students even. In fact, he decided he loved women so much he wanted to become one, and once he became one she just kept on loving women.'

'Well, she certainly makes a notable babe.'

'It doesn't bother you?'

'No, why should it?'

'Do you really mean that?'

'Of course. It's none of my business, and it's hardly exotic any more – you can read about it in the newspapers all the time.'

She leaned across and kissed me.

'I'm so relieved, I thought I'd caused my usual chaos. I mean that fight was bad enough, but ...'

'If you don't mind my asking, what was the fight about? I

couldn't quite figure out the alliances. What was Ilse She-Wolf of the SS all steamed up about?'

'Well, Marie-Claire, that's her name, she was jealous because she knew I used to be close to Hymie when he was still a man, so she thought I was trying to start it up again.'

'So she's a jealous woman.'

Gudrun studied her coffee.

'Well, yes and no – she's very broad-minded – in some ways.'

She actually blushed.

'I think I'll forbear further enquiries.'

I found I wasn't surprised. Since Gudrun had had an affair with Hymie, I suppose she wondered about the new Heidi, and if Marie-Claire was part of the bargain, so much the better.

'But not as broad-minded as you,' she cooed.

'Oh, I just …'

'And I haven't thanked you.'

So she thanked me.

Ten

Why, how very black and cross you look! And how – how funny and grim!

Doris Hippo's face beamed round the door frame:
   'One word – *aromatherapy*!'
   'Harrison doesn't allow …'
   'I know, but just take this brochure …'
   I took it and she left. As November passes and the term winds down, the correcting is becoming oppressive. Harrison seems to be taking his naps at home more and more, and what little evidence I have of him comes from the occasional note on my desk, the following clipped to a sheet of administrative drivel:

   And that literary nuisance, who just now is rather rife,
   The deconstructionist – I've got him on the list!
   All funny fellows, comic men, and clowns of college life –
   They'd none of 'em be missed – they'd none of 'em be missed.

However, he also left me a teach-yourself-Icelandic book which I looked into one Sunday afternoon during a break. After making allowances for the peculiar letters for 'th', I could see that some words were obvious cognates – móðir, faðir, dóttir, bróðir – but what was I to make of mjög (very), leikkona (actress) and gerðu svo vel (please)? I decided to leave it until the Christmas holidays.
   hekladottir@postnet.dk did send me a characteristic e-mail a few weeks after her visit:

will/ i suppose you look down on insurence salesmen too, I mean like I used to, but I sure am glad my landlord had fire insurance because otherwise it would have been a total disaster, but it wasn't my fault, really it wasn't, something about the wiring, and I lost all my clothes except what I was wearing, you try standing around at three in the morning in Denmark in November

« 65 »

with a coat pulled over your nightdress while your house burns down, anyway, the insurince paid me thousands of kroner, don't ask about the exchange rate, and thanks to thor most of my papers were in my office at the university except some that this really nice firemen got for me the next day from the wreck they were scorched but they didnt burn because it seems paper is hard to burn and of course the thesis is on disk and also on my office computer, I havent had a minute to work on it this fall, so with all those kroner, they paid off as if I had bought the clothes at danish prices, about ten times can prices, so I came out ahead, so whats wrong with being accident prone Mr smartypants?

Anyway thanks for being such a good host when i visited, im sure glad i didn't burn down your house.

Anyway im going to be busy over the holidays so I wont write again so god jule as they say here, the breweries put out a special beer called julol but I don't like it much its heavy but you might.

Love and kisses,

Gudrun heppinn (the lucky) descendant of leif the lucky!

I contemplated a scorch mark one of her cigarettes left in my carpet and shuddered.

My other romantic interest, if that is not too enthusiastic a term, also seems to be going nowhere. Two Fridays ago, I happened to be in the office when Margaret returned from class. Faute de mieux (I'm picking up some French) I suggested happy hour and dinner again. She said she would like to, but she and Julia had some sort of McGill dinner meeting. If I was interested she could she meet me about ten. She arrived in a cab half an hour late, looking very seductive. A week or so later we saw *Bridget Jones's Diary*. An enjoyable evening which we agreed to do again soon, but when I telephoned a few days later I got her answering machine and she hasn't called back. I give up – enough of the Black Death.

And although I teach in her department and live in her house, I have seen little of my landlady since the party. I once encountered her outside her office, but she excused herself from pleasantries because she had a meeting; at home, I slip my rent cheque through her mail slot, and I can't be bothered watching her comings and goings through the little window in the bathroom.

However, the occasional coincidence of social noises from above, along with the presence of the limousine at the front door, suggests visits from her lady friend. Curious, I asked Harrison.

'So who is Ilse the She-Wolf? I can imagine a rich lawyer driving a fancy car herself, but a chauffeured limo – it doesn't make sense.'

'My, you are slow, Ensign Ass. In fact, Marie-Claire's not a lawyer or doctor by profession, but, as I recall, a journalist. However, at the moment she holds down the position of Quebec Minister for the Purity of the Blood of the People of the Sacred Flame of the Old Stump or whatever it's called this month.'

'Our chair keeps exalted company.'

'Indeed.'

'Do all provincial ministers have chauffeured limousines?'

'Ever since the then premier and his sweet patootsie ran over a derelict in the small hours.'

'Really? I expect he was in a certain amount of trouble for that one.'

'On the contrary – the fuzz astutely administered a breathalyser to the corpse. He was declared to be drunk, and had perversely stepped into the path of the oncoming car bearing our perfectly innocent, perfectly sober premier and his perfectly innocent, perfectly sober patootsie, so premier and patootsie went home and slept the sleep of the just. But from then on he used a chauffeured limousine, and so do they all, all honourable men and women.'

'That can't be true?'

'You could look it up. But don't bother, I beg you, because it just gets loonier. Those of us who live here stay to wonder at the latest manifestation. Read Mordecai. Read the dreary Austen novel by that drudge at the other college. You'll either get used to it, or step in front of a car, or get yourself a nice low enrolment tenure-track position in a university with temperate climate, relaxed liquor laws, low taxes, an international airport nearby, and hordes of compliant, scantily clad babes who don't splice with commas.'

'No, really, I am interested.'

'I hate Emily Brontë!'

'What now?'

'I hate Emily Brontë and every other nineteenth-century romantic peddler of passion. Let's all climb to the top of Wuthering Heights and swear to love one another for life and beyond the grave, never mind how many other lives we destroy, let's moon over moonlight glowing on a ruined castle, purpose-built only last year for mooning, let's be obsessive in our love, implacable in our hatred, let's stand on a windswept crag overlooking a stormy ocean and bawl poetic thoughts into the teeth of the tempest, let's all go crazy. But most of all, let's get passionate about the soul of the nation, let's …'

'But Emily Brontë wasn't a nationalist; there's no nationalism at all in her novel.'

'Who do you want – Wagner? Hegel? Fichte? It's all cut from the same cloth, where's your cultural and literary history? Romanticism means feeling over intellect, identification with nature, ersatz antiques, night, storm, sea, and when it gets political, a bogus history demanding identification with our ethnic brethren and sistren, and concomitant hatred of all who are not us.'

'Yes, but …'

'I hold Emily Brontë personally responsible for Ilse She-Wolf of the SS, and all her sadistic kind.'

'Surely that's …'

'What gift did Catherine Earnshaw, a moppet of five or six, ask her father to bring her from Liverpool?'

'It's been a while since I read *Wuthering Heights*.'

'A whip.'

'That's interesting, but …'

'Consider by contrast the Right Honourable Sir Joseph Porter, KCB, First Lord of the Admiralty:

> 'Of legal knowledge I acquired such a grip
> That they took me into the partnership.
> And that junior partnership, I ween,
> Was the only ship that I ever had seen.'

'Pirates of Penzance?'
'Pinafore:

'But that ship so suited me,
That now I am the ruler of the Queen's Navee.

'Any nationalism more bellicose than that and you've got storm troopers ramping about the streets and jackboots tracking mud across the wall-to-wall. Of course, like Marie-Claire, Emily never killed anyone, great writer though she was, but she was a typical romantic who dreamed of sadism, murder, necrophilia. By contrast, Egil Skallagrímsson, a consummate classicist, slaughtered dozens, hundreds, but always for honour or loot, never for Icelandic or Norwegian nationalism. Thus endeth the first lesson.'

Argument with Harrison is inevitably fruitless. His magpie mind jumps about among such strange and unexpected items that while I can follow him, I will never be able to lead him.

He paused at the door.

'I should never have become a teacher, I should have been ... a pirate king.'

'How romantic.'

'Entirely pragmatic:

'When I sally forth to seek my prey
I help myself in the royal way ...

'But it's not the piracy itself that appeals, Ensign Ass – looting, burning and pillaging – though Egil made a fortune at it. No, I would expect to be redeemed by the love of a beautiful woman. Salvation through bonking.'

'I thought you'd been redeemed enough times already.'

'Four or five marriages are not redemption but perdition.'

'Four or five? Aren't you sure?'

'Could be six. Depends on how you count them.'

Eleven

After playing lady's maid ... putting my cakes in the oven, and making the house and kitchen cheerful with great fires befitting Christmas-eve, I prepared to sit down and amuse myself by singing.

Let me dress you smart.

I was eyeing a morose stack of final exams when Ringo Toadie materialized in the doorway.

'I wonder if you've ever considered hand puppets?'

His T-shirt deplored machines.

'No.'

'To engage students in literature at the post-secondary level?'

He displayed a thick booklet. The cover sported puppets of Heathcliff and Catherine, Poe and his raven, Mrs Tiggy-Winkle and Jemima Puddle-Duck.

'This gives the ABCs of adapting your courses to hand puppets? And there's a questionnaire? For when ...'

'No.'

'But it's for my doctoral thesis?'

'I'm expecting Harrison any minute.'

He thrust the booklet into my hand and was gone.

'And stay away!' I heard Harrison call. 'Welcome to the week of the dying grandmothers,' he announced as he dropped a bag of exams on his desk. 'Welcome to the week of obscure religious festivals which prohibit all writing on pain of excommunication, the week of diseases exacerbated by term papers but soothed by all-night raves, the week of devilish web viruses which download chunks of readers' guides but refuse to allow quotation marks or citations.'

'The week of I never met an excuse I didn't like.'

'The week of,' solemnly, 'the dog ate my hard drive.'

He slumped in his chair.

'So how did you find your students?'

'They were usually waiting in the classroom.'

'That should be my line.'

'They're just as you and Margaret said – good kids on the whole and likely no worse than the ones Socrates taught.'

'At least no worse than the Westmount tennis players whose essays I corrected when I was in third year at McGill. By the way, I've promoted you to lieutenant for getting through the term alive. And reasonably sane.'

'Why, thank you.'

'What are you doing for Christmas?'

'I was thinking of visiting my folks in Nova Scotia, but the airfare, even with my salary ... And when I did call, everything was booked. So I decided to hole up in my flat working on a piece on Icelandic influences in Smallweed.'

'What influences?'

'None.'

'Well, if that becomes too masochistic, drop round Chez Morgan for Christmas dinner. I am a decent cook. One of the arts of the civilized man.'

'Thank you, Harrison – it's most thoughtful.'

'Dr Taylor will also be there.'

What now?

The delights of the fiction of Augustus Smallweed have been a meagre reward for the three months of student prose. I've been through all Smallweed's work several times, but wanted to refresh my memory of certain passages in his so-called comic masterpiece, the excruciatingly unfunny *Prairie Oysters*. But the dining room chairs are too uncomfortable for long periods of reading, and when I lie on the couch I find myself falling asleep within minutes. So I've done my Christmas shopping instead.

In Edinburgh I discovered that museum shops offer a variety of reasonably tasteful gifts, some at prices I can afford, and the shop at the Montreal Museum of Fine Arts is no exception. After some deliberation I bought a flashy pair of dangly earrings in red and black enamel for Ms Felsen. For Harrison I found a Gilbert and Sullivan calendar with reproductions of posters for each month and annotations of premieres, birthdays, and such. That, along with a good bottle of straight malt – another thing I learned about in Edinburgh – should suffice.

I'm not quite sure why Harrison mentioned Margaret is coming as well – I've had enough of her on-again-off-again – but on impulse I did another tour of the jewellery counter. Silver, probably, given that she always wears black. And there was just the thing, a silver necklace and earring set, in elongated rectangles, inspired by Charles Rennie Macintosh and done on licence from the Burrell Collection in Glasgow. It was more than I wanted to spend on someone as chilly as Margaret, but it seemed perfect.

This afternoon, Christmas Eve, I could tell from the footsteps above that Ms Felsen was home, so rang her doorbell.

She was a long time coming to the door and seemed distracted when she did. She was in her oriental silk robe. Tinker Bell, however, was decked out for the season with red and green ribbons.

'Oh, thanks,' she said when I handed her the black package. 'You'll have to forgive me, I didn't think to get you anything, but come in and share some Christmas spirit. What's a Christmas spirit, Tinker Bell? Perhaps a vodka martini with a wedge of lime and a cherry?'

However distracted she gets, Heidi is always on top of the drinks.

'A plain gin and tonic will do for me, thanks.'

'Here's to peace on earth, good will to men.'

'Good Will – that's you.'

'And women,' I replied in what I hoped was the politically correct spirit.

'And everyone in between, though since September the eleventh, I'm not so sure about some of them,' Heidi added. 'I suppose they've told you about me? About my operations?'

'It wasn't gossip. Someone let it slip.'

'Gudrun, of course. But it doesn't matter – I'm surprised Harrison didn't tell you straight off. Curious? Titillated? Shocked?'

'Christine Jorgensen made the change fifty years ago.'

'Bless you, Will.'

She leaned forward and kissed my cheek.

'But let's see what the thoughtful gentleman got his landlady for

Christmas ... Ohh, they're just darling, very art nouveau retro chic.'

'Is that what they are?'

'Very then, very now. They'll go perfectly with the red and black cocktail frock I bought for Christmas. I'd model it for you now, but réveillon isn't for hours.'

'Pardon?'

'Christmas Eve party. I wonder ...'

She stared at the ceiling, then looked at me with a naughty smile.

'I wonder if I can show you Marie-Claire's gift to me?'

I shrugged.

'As you wish.'

'You seem ... liberal minded enough to ...'

'Oh, if it's private, you needn't ...'

I was expecting sexy undies, or an explicitly illustrated edition of Sappho.

'I can't bear it, I'm so proud of them, I just have to show them off. Close your eyes.'

What now?

After a rustle of silk, Heidi said, 'Open them!'

She had let the robe slip from her shoulders, exposing her breasts.

'What do you think?' she asked eagerly.

Each nipple was pierced with a gold ring.

'Marie-Claire paid for the appointment and for the rings. They're mainly decorative, with just a hint of BDSM. Don't you just adore them?'

'Ye-yes,' I stammered. 'Very chic.'

'I was so afraid it was going to hurt, but it didn't really. Well, the left one did a bit, but I didn't feel the right one at all.' She leaned forward and flipped the rings. 'They're still tender because they were only done three days ago, and I have to keep turning them through like this so they don't get stuck, and there's a solution for bathing the nipples so they heal properly. I'm so proud of them. Here, you try.'

She flipped them again to demonstrate.

'I don't think ...'

'Oh, don't be such a prude!'

Trying not to touch the flesh, I lifted each ring a fraction of an inch.

'They're heavier than I expected.'

'Twenty-two-carat gold – Marie-Claire always insists on the best.'

'Yes, they're very pretty. Very tasteful.'

'I'm thinking about getting a chain with clasps at the ends to attach to each ring, so that it hangs across – it wouldn't go with the bustier, but with no bra and a plunging neckline, it would be striking, don't you think?'

'Very.'

'But I wonder …' She hooked one of her new earrings to a ring. 'This is another decorative possibility.' She went to mirror by the door, turning one way and the other.

'A bit de trop, I think, the enamel doesn't go with the gold.'

'Yes, I think smaller ones would …'

'Well, the possibilities are endless. Of course, everyone's getting piercings these days, especially the students – half the girls have their navels done, and from what I hear in the powder room, a lot of them have their nipples done too. I won't tell you about Marie-Claire's piercings – they're private, aren't they, Tinker Bell.'

I glanced at my watch. 'Right, well, I've got to …'

'I've shocked you!'

'No, really, I have a lot to do. And be assured I do I feel privileged to have seen your rings.'

'How about the boobs, eh?'

'They're magnificent.'

'Forty-two C, and no flop to them.' She jiggled them from side to side. 'You won't find tits like this on a fifty-six-year-old broad every day.'

'No, I expect not.'

I opened the front door.

'Though when you think of it, they're only about a year and a half old.'

'I hadn't thought of that.'

'Well then, you ought to be ashamed of yourself – you've been ogling the tits of a fourteen-year-old!'

Twelve

There, there, children – to your seats!

Mr Earnshaw carved bountiful platefuls.

I did not call her unfeeling long.

We got rid of all gloom in the excitement of the exercise, and our pleasure was increased by the arrival of the Gimmerton band, mustering fifteen strong: a trumpet, a trombone, clarionets, bassoons, French horns, and a bass viol, besides singers. They go the rounds of all the respectable houses, and … we esteemed it a first-rate treat to hear them.

After the usual carols had been sung, we set them to songs and glees.

Harrison lives down the hill below Sherbrooke Street. His brick row house is not as grand as Ms Felsen's, but with ten or eleven rooms is grander than anything I can aspire to in the foreseeable. Although lights shone in the front room and the hall, and although I could hear the bell ringing, no one came to let me in, so I tried the door and found it unlocked.

I wished season's greetings to four or five people talking in the living room, strangers all.

'… wishing I had the body of Angelina Jolie and the mind of Margaret Atwood,' one woman was saying, 'but I got the reverse.'

'You said it, babe, not me,' a bearded man replied.

'And a merry Christmas to you, too, Harv!'

I could see Harrison standing at the dining-room table with a silver spoon in one hand and a flute of champagne in the other.

'Gleðileg jól, Lieutenant Ass,' he called. 'Find yourself a glass,' waving vaguely, 'and a drink to put in it.'

Behind him was a woman in a red dress, and beyond her, in the kitchen, several giggling girls. Despite his remarks about various ex-wives, he had not spoken of a current woman in his life. When I got to the dining room, however, I saw that the woman was Margaret, nearly unrecognizable without her customary black. And her customary reserve.

'Merry Christmas, Will,' she chirped, and surprised me with a hug and a Montrealer's two-cheek kiss. 'And let me just get your present – I left it with my coat.'

'These are for you, Harrison. Sorry I didn't wrap them, but the paper would have cost more than this one,' handing him the calendar, 'and the shape makes the bottle obvious.'

'Thank you very much,' he murmured. While he was silently turning the pages of the calendar, Margaret returned with a neatly wrapped box. Inside was a glass pot with a stainless steel top and plunger, and a bag of coffee from a chic Westmount shop.

'For café pression. Promise me – no more instant.'

'I promise. And this is for you, Margaret. The woman said if you don't like it, you can exchange it for something else.'

'Ohh, the MMFA Shop,' she said as she opened the box. 'Charles Rennie Macintosh – how appropriate, coming from an Edinburgher.'

'It's Edimbourgeois, and he was Glasgow, but it's close enough. And they seemed to be in your taste.'

'They are, and they're lovely, just lovely.'

When she kissed me, I thought I could see tears starting in her eyes, but concluded I must be wrong.

'Congrats, Lieutenant Ass, they like exchanging presents – it gives them an excuse to shop, the pinnacle of intellectual achievement for persons of their gender persuasion, and not least for the Black Death here. Or are you the Red Death tonight? Where's your masque?'

'Harrison, why don't I find a carving knife and alter your gender persuasion?'

'Go ahead, top drawer right – and then I'd be able to attend departmental meetings.'

I tried to sense if Margaret was there as Harrison's companion, as mine, or on her own. I soon saw that she was directing her remarks, her smiles, her touches equally. I also saw that she was watching her drinking, barely sipping the champagne. She was also watching her tongue. With her red dress and matching lipstick, her flashing blue eyes, and glistening black hair, she was stunningly beautiful. And winsome, especially when she snuggled up to me with her head on my shoulder, and nuzzled my cheek: 'He's a beast, isn't he, Will? You'll protect me from him, won't you?'

'Beware, Lieutenant Ass, for as Field Marshal Gilbert puts it,

> 'In all the woes that curse our race,
> There is a lady in the case.'

'Named Portia, no doubt, because she's the only one smart enough to understand the law, don't you agree, Will?'

She snuggled against me again.

'Unhand that innocent guest, you harpy, and begone!'

'Exit stage right.'

I wasn't entirely convinced by this teasing, beguiling Margaret, but she drifted away to mingle and I thought I should do the same. When, half an hour later, we did sit to table, we were twelve, and I had acquainted myself with five or six besides Harrison and Margaret. They were a diverse lot – a history professor each from McGill and Concordia, both women, and their husbands, one a dentist who skis; a poet who perforce makes her living teaching; a part-owner of an audio-video business; a lawyer and his pediatrician wife, who have a sailboat and for whom Harrison used to crew. The three pretty young women from the kitchen who now clustered about the host's end of the table were, I assumed, former students. So much for all the claims about Harrison's integrity.

Margaret surprised me by taking the seat next to mine.

What now?

'Surely an appropriate motif to honour the birth of Jesus,' she murmured, nodding toward the three girls with Harrison, 'miniskirts and plunging necklines.'

'And push-up bras.'

'And fishnet stay-ups.'

'And giggles.'

'And thong panties.'

'Are you sure, Margaret?'

'No VPL.'

Was the booze loosening her tongue?

But the booze was loosening everyone's tongue. The party had some of the usual trappings – red and green streamers about the walls, evergreen boughs with red bows, crackers and paper hats. But the music was not carols by King's College or the Vienna Boys' Choir – Harrison had a CD player with a carousel, and with his remote directed it to play highlights from Gilbert and Sullivan. He also handed out photocopied song sheets (I've got mine here) and every few minutes we all had to join in. We began with the chorus of peers from *Iolanthe*:

> 'Bow, bow, ye lower middle classes!
> Bow, bow, ye tradesmen, bow, ye masses!
> Blow the trumpets, bang the brasses!
> Tantantara! Tzing! Boom!'

'Not exactly the Christmas spirit either,' I remarked to Margaret. 'Not something reflecting "Good King Wenceslas" or "Away in a Manager".'

'Or "While Shepherds Watched". But perhaps "We Three Kings" approaches the spirit.'

After a fine bouillabaisse, the three fattest men did a falsetto 'Climbing over rocky mountain,' from *The Pirates of Penzance*, camping outrageously on 'We'll be queens, and make decrees.' After the salad of mâche and sautéed pear with red dressing for seasonal colour, the women were handed doughnuts and lowered their voices for 'A policeman's lot is not a happy one.'

'Why the opposite sex singing?' I asked Margaret.

'I think it's his notion that in Quebec everything – all law, all logic, all human behaviour – is topsy-turvy.'

'And the doughnuts?'

'Ever seen a Quebec cop?'

Just before the main course, while the guests did the choruses, Harrison led with considerable talent and verve the Mikado's:

'My object all sublime
I shall achieve in time –
To let the punishment fit the crime –
The punishment fit the crime;'

Between courses we were encouraged to walk about to whet the appetite, or to enjoy a smoke – Harrison himself clamped a small cigar between his teeth as he supervised the young women in the cooking. His claim to be a good cook was justified by the meal, and the main course was duckling – half a dozen of them – along with wild rice, red cabbage and chestnut, and anise. When I put it to him that he was exploiting the innocent youth of his three assistants, he replied,

'Hardly innocent, Lieutenant Ass, if you're talking about these three tarts.'

The three giggled and pummelled him.

'Harrison, how dare you insult students?'

'They are three little maids from school, Megs, but that's hardly the operative relationship. Ladies and gentlemen, those who don't already know them, may I introduce my daughters – Faith, Hope and Charity.'

'Dad!' they chorused.

'Humility, Prudence and Divine Discontent?'

'Dad!'

'Don't tax my memory. To the best of my recollection, their mother named them for characters in TV soap operas or sitcoms or something. Take your pick. Tiffany? Stephanie? Melody?'

At last they introduced themselves: Elizabeth, Emma and Anne.

'The names of Jane Austen's favourite heroines,' Elizabeth explained.

'I told you I hate Emily Brontë,' Harrison added, 'but I didn't tell you I love Jane Austen.'

Margaret was flabbergasted.

'Well, they confirm it,' I said.

As the daughters were removing the main course debris, Harrison called us all to stand to sing 'Never mind the why and wherefore' from *Pinafore*. With interspersed solo lines and repeats, it is a complicated exercise and we kept making mistakes. Unfortunately, Harrison insisted every error be paid for with a mouthful of wine which doubtless caused more mistakes. Margaret, who had the part of Josephine, was a particular victim because she kept confusing her lines, 'And a *tar* who ploughs the water' and 'For a gallant captain's daughter'. When she descended to 'And a *tar* who ploughs the daughter', Harrison dimmed the lights, and called for the plum pudding.

The shortest daughter bore in a flaming pudding, the second a bowl of a white sauce, and the tallest a tray with a bottle of port and glasses. After serving, they stood giggling by the electronic equipment.

'Girls,' called Harrison, 'Not tonight.'

'Oh, Dad, don't be so silly – it's our present to everyone.'

'Ladies and gentlemen, for what we are about to receive, my apologies. In partial explanation, they live with their mother – in Vancouver.'

Anne fiddled with the CD remote, gave a cue, and they began to sing 'Three little maids from school.' But after the short opening chorus, when each gets a line, they began to vamp, lifting their skirts, bending forward to show their cleavage, and undoing buttons and snaps.

Harrison lifted his hands in resignation. 'You try stopping them,' he mouthed.

The CD player was set to repeat, and by the third repeat, they were waving their bras above their heads:

> 'Three little maids who, all unwary,
> Come from a ladies' seminary,
> Freed from its genius tutelary –
>   Three little maids from school!'

I scanned the faces of the other guests. 'Margaret,' I murmured, 'No one seems in the least offended.'

'It's Quebec,' she replied.

> 'Pert as a school-girl well can be
> Filled to the brim with girlish glee,
>   Three little maids from school!'

They did not remove their stockings or their panties, contenting themselves with flashing their bottoms at us:

ELIZABETH: Everything is a source of fun.
EMMA: Nobody's safe, for we care for none!
ANNE: Life is a joke that's just begun!
THE THREE: Three little maids from school!

They bowed demurely, exited to enthusiastic applause, and returned clothed.

'I hope you're satisfied, poppets, at the distress you've visited on our guests.'

'Don't be silly, Dad!'

'Oh, Dad, don't spoil the fun!'

'Anyway, now it's over!'

'You see? Minds, such as they are, of their own. However, let us have back the immortals.'

He flourished his remote and G and S resumed.

But a number of guests, both men and women, chatted with the girls and from what I could hear congratulated and thanked them.

Margaret smiled ruefully.

'I told you they were wearing thong panties,' she said.

'I defer to your superior perception.'

'By the way, have you heard they've invented a bra to go with thong panties?'

'Really?'

'It's called the Bob Hope Bra – the jingle is "Thongs for the Mammaries".'

'You didn't make that up.'

'Oh, but I did,' she simpered.

'You know, Margaret, this performance was … indicative somehow. Look, once in Edmonton, a bunch of us went on a pub crawl for end of term or something. One of the places had a wet T-shirt contest – girls from the audience. They didn't, of course, take their tops off – well, one girl flashed them for a second – but the guys in the room were howling like wolves, barking like dogs, grunting like pigs – they were reduced to animals. It was gross, disgusting, demeaning. I was embarrassed for the women because it seemed to me they had done it in a spirit of fun and generosity, and they were humiliated in return. But tonight people were respectful. They didn't make it demeaning or dirty. It was, well, just fun and generosity. At least I thought so.'

'I think you are altogether too benevolent to be believable.'

'I'm just trying to be honest about what I saw, what I felt.'

Margaret gazed at me doubtfully.

'Do you really mean that? What I see is what I get? Plain white bread?'

'I live in Montreal now – can't I be a baguette at least?'

'Your candour suggests seven grain whole wheat.'

'Sounds more like Harrison.'

'No, he's sourdough.'

Harrison called us to order while he sang the Captain's song from *Pinafore*, and we sang our questions:

> 'What never?
> No, never!
> What, *never?*
> Well, hardly ever!'

He followed this with the Admiral's 'I am the monarch of the sea' with the women doing the chorus, 'And we are his sisters, and his cousins, and his aunts' with its ensemble reprise. Next Harrison did the admiral's patter song, 'When I was a lad I served a term.' These together with the patter chorus took us at least half an hour to get right, with practice improving our performance and the digestifs degrading it. By the end, Margaret and I were embracing as we roared out the final,

> 'Stick close to your desks and never go to sea,
> And you all may be Rulers of the Queen's Navee!'

Any attempt to go on was impossible. Half the company wandered off in search of toilets or softer seating, while the rest of us stayed at the table in small groups, three or four gathered around Harrison and working on G and S, other groups about their raucous business. Margaret rested her head on my shoulder.

'I'm not drunk, Will, at least not very drunk, but I'm so tired I'll probably fall asleep on the stairs. Can you help me home?'

An innocent request, I was convinced – she was certainly sleepy.

I was in a group at the front door donning coats when I glanced back to the kitchen. Margaret was saying goodbye to Harrison in a lingering clinch.

Taxis were impossible, but the sailors dropped us at Margaret's door. When I paused, she held my arm.

'I'd offer to invite you up for a coffee or a night-cap, Will, but ...'

'I'm sleepy too, Margaret.'

She kissed me on the cheeks, then murmured something.

'Sorry, I didn't catch ...'

'Follie ... sempre libera,' she replied. 'It's from an opera. I'm ... I don't think I'm ready for anything long term just now.'

'I wasn't proposing anything.'

'No, you weren't, were you.'

A long, tight embrace.

'You're sweet,' she said. 'Sometime perhaps I'll explain.'

'No explanations necessary.'

She studied me. After what seemed a very long time, she said, 'Well ... good night.'

Thirteen

They *do* live more in earnest, more in themselves, and less in surface change, and frivolous external things. I could fancy a love for life here almost possible.

And she went up in the dark; I followed.

The clock is on the stroke of eleven, sir.

On Boxing Day, with considerable nervousness, I left a message on Margaret's answering machine:

'Hi, it's Will. We didn't speak of it, but I'm at loose ends for New Year's Eve. If you're interested in getting together, you have my number.'

She returned the call the next afternoon, explaining that Julia and her husband had already invited her to a dinner party on the West Island. 'It's sit-down, so no extra guests. But I'm free on the second. What did you have in mind?'

I had been thinking about dinner and drinks, perhaps a movie, but hadn't been able to find anything interesting in the paper. Margaret pointed out that many restaurants were likely to be closed, and the open ones sepulchral.

'In that case, Margaret, I'm not much of a cook, but I'm willing to give it a try if you'll take the chance.'

It was a culinary adventure in a life which has rarely dared more than the grilled cheese sandwich:

- a dish of almonds on the coffee table when she arrived;
- a ham with rings of canned pineapple stuck on with cloves and with a cherry in the middle, just as my mother does it;

« 87 »

- mashed potatoes – lumpy; when I pressed her, Margaret said I might buy a potato masher;
- boiled carrots;
- green salad with Paul Newman dressing – pulling out all stops to impress; when I asked her, Margaret admitted I might buy a salad spinner to wash the greens – 'and no more iceberg lettuce';
- a fancy Italian cake called panettone from an Italian deli, a tribute not to my cooking skills, but to my frugality – it was half price;
- café pression made with the pot Margaret gave me for Christmas;
- a choice of wines – Chilean, Australian, Californian; cognac.

Frankly, I rather enjoyed the effort. Margaret was certainly polite in her praises, and was gentle with the advice about glazing the ham, adding butter, sugar and tarragon (I wrote it down) to the carrots, baking the potatoes, mashing the white, then putting the mash back in the jackets with a bit of Parmesan – 'and not the grated stuff in the can – you have to buy good Parmesan and grate it only as you need it.' She also suggested three or four easy but interesting salads and a dressing called vinaigrette I can make myself. And educated me about wines:

'With ham a white is perhaps better, a Chablis or Pouilly-Fuissé. You can serve red, but it should be light. Cabernet Sauvignon is more appropriate with steak or game. A Pinot Noir from Burgundy or a Beaujolais are better with ham, so that's why, when you offered me the choice, I picked the Shiraz which the Australians ...'

In fact, we (well, mostly she) spent several hours talking about cooking and serving food and wine. She was full of praise for Harrison's cooking, although she admitted the service tended to be a bit slapdash.

'But that's all part of the casual tone of his ménage.'

'Just as lumpy potatoes and sandy lettuce are part of mine.'

'You'll learn; you have the right attitude.'

'There's hope for me?'

'Oh, there's nothing wrong with your style that practice and money can't fix. Such as expanding your collection of CDs beyond *Greatest Light Classical Hits*, *Best of the Big Bands*, and *Candlelight Reverie.*'

'Yes, well, I couldn't afford more than one every month or three.'

'Now you can, you just need someone to teach you.'

Just too late I realized I should have eschewed the obvious come-on of, 'Will you teach me?' while leaning forward and batting eyelashes at her, because Margaret pulled back slightly and said, 'We'll see.'

I made a penitent show of getting the dirty dishes stacked. Margaret joined me in the kitchenette, ran a finger down the line of my jaw.

'I'm sorry, Will. Sometimes I'm a bit quick with the trigger finger.'

'That's okay, Margaret. I did notice you're wearing the necklace and earrings.'

'They are perfect, aren't they? Let me make it up to you – we'll do the dishes together, then we'll go to my place for another coffee and I'll begin your musical education. Is it a deal?'

I wandered into her living room while she strode to the kitchen with the sure step of someone on her own turf. Her black dress flattered her trim figure, and her legs were slim and elegant in black stockings and simple shoes with two-inch heels.

'Black becomes you,' I called.

'Dress or mood?'

'Are you being sensitive or perverse?'

'Just playing with words. Coffee or something stronger?'

'Coffee sounds fine.'

While the water was coming to the boil, she went to the bedroom. Her apartment looked just as neat and austere as it had on my earlier visit – no Christmas decorations, not even the usual line of cards on the mantelpiece. I noticed the brush strokes on the paintings – they were real, not reproductions. And the furniture and accessories all looked expensive. Margaret obviously did not shop at IKEA, Swedish for 'the grad student's friend.' How long had she been at the college? Three years? I am earning far more than I ever have before, but my bank balance isn't growing fast enough for this stuff.

Margaret returned with her lipstick freshened and her hair brushed.

'Do you like that one?' she asked, indicating the painting over the mantelpiece.

'Very much. Restful ... balanced.'

'Yes, as well as sane and congenial. That's why I have it there. And why I call it David Hume.'

The kettle clicked and she went to complete the coffee.

'Easy to live with, I expect,' I called.

'Yes. And that's why that one behind the couch is behind the couch – so I don't have to look it while I'm reading or eating. I only see it when I look at it deliberately.'

It was an uneasy composition mainly of dark blue and purple.

'Kierkegaard?'

'Good guess, but it's Schopenhauer.'

'And the black and grey one over the dining room table? Marx?'

'I haven't quite decided yet,' handing me my cup, 'but I think it's Descartes. I didn't buy that one so much for the idea as to match the furniture.'

'What's one step above trailer trash?'

Margaret licked her fingertip and marked one up for me. After a little thought she put on a CD of a woman singing lilting music in German.

'Elizabeth Schwarzkopf's desert island disc of highlights from Viennese operetta. Surprised?'

My mind scurried about for an answer.

'Well ...'

'Your pause betrays you. I know you think me cold and rational, because that's how students and people in the department think of me, but the rational Margaret is the pose – the real Margaret is hopelessly sentimental. At least I think I have it right way round. I'm not always sure.'

With a slight smile on her lips, she gazed at me in silence as the singer's voice swelled.

'I can hear something in French – chambre séparée? – but the other words are in German.'

'A chambre séparée is a room at a ball or theatre where couples could sit out a dance in private.'

She lifted her cup a few inches in a toast.

'To privacy.'

'To privacy,' I said.

'And to dancing. Shall we?'

'I've never waltzed, I've hardly ever danced, come to that.'

'I'll teach you,' taking my hand.

I didn't learn to waltz, but I didn't stumble or step on her feet either, for Margaret held herself lightly to me, and let her body move with mine.

'This next one isn't a waltz,' she said, 'so perhaps we should retire to our chambre séparée.'

I took the chair; she slipped off her shoes and stretched out on the couch.

'So you're actually going to Iceland with Harrison?' she asked, reaching for her coffee cup.

'So it seems. I still have a month or so before I have to send the deposit, and a month or two after that before I buy the airline ticket.'

'Expensive, I expect.'

'I don't feel rich, but I expect I can afford it. I mean, you've only been at it for three years, and look what you've got.'

She glanced about the room.

'I've been thrifty. Are you going on to Europe from Iceland? I understand the add-ons to Europe are cheap.'

'As good as free. They fly to Glasgow, so I've been considering Edinburgh. Or perhaps London. And I have had some hints about some documents at the University of Sussex.'

'Sounds interesting.'

'Why don't you come too? If you feel like it, I mean.'

'I'll think about it.'

The music was lilting again, but the conversation had moved a long way from the waltz.

'And what would you do in Edinburgh?'

'Just see old friends.' Surely she wasn't wondering about a girl-friend? 'I don't think I can unearth any more on Smallweed there, but I lived there for two years, so I know a lot of people. And a lot of pubs.'

'The Abbotsford. The Cafe Royal. Bennet's. Sandy Bell's. The Oxford. The Diggers.'

'How long were you in Edinburgh?'

'Two weeks during the Festival a few years ago.'

'You must have worked at it. Any tourist can find the Cafe Royal and the Abbotsford, but the others take some searching.'

'Deep digging, especially for the Diggers when Hearts aren't playing.'

'Or sleuthing to find the Oxford.'

She pointed to a line of Ian Rankin mysteries in the bookcase – his Inspector John Rebus is a regular in the Oxford.

'I suppose Miss Hekla will be in Reykjavik.'

'She says she will, but she's a mite disorganized.'

'Only when the bill comes.'

'Meow.'

'Or with other people's health, property and peace of mind.'

'I sense a long and painful story.'

'Not so long.'

'Therefore painful. A story that's none of my business.'

She gazed into the distance. At last she held out her hand.

'Something else I may tell you sometime. Let's dance.'

Again she moved lightly against me, but not as close this time, for she seemed distracted, thinking of Gudrun perhaps, of whatever Gudrun had done. Then she began to sing along:

> 'Doch klüger ist's, mann wird geliebt,
> Statt dass man selber Liebe gibt,
> Beherrscht die Situation als die Herrin ganz leicht.'

The next piece lilted and Margaret's mood softened as we moved about the carpet, though the light, the hint of her perfume ...

'It's about the Müllerin, the mill girl who spurns a humble fisherman who loves her because she thinks she can do better:

> 'Sei nicht bös, es kann nicht sein
> Sei nicht bös, und schick dich drein ...
> Don't be angry, it cannot be;
> Don't be angry, just accept it ...

THIRTEEN

'She goes proudly out into the world, but in time returns, proud no longer. She calls to the fisherman, but he replies:

'Sei nicht bös, es kann nicht sein ...

'Yes, well ... The next is not really for dancing, but it has a nice refrain:

'Meine Lippen, sie küssen so heiss,
Meine Glieder sind schmiegsam und weiss,
In den Sternen, da steht es geschreiben,
Du sollst küssen, du sollst lieben!'

'Which means?'
'I'll photocopy the lyrics for you. Roughly, "My lips kiss so hot, my limbs are so supple and white, in the stars it's written that you must kiss me, you must love me".'
She kissed me lightly, and we danced.
'But the last song is perhaps the best; you'll probably recognize it.'
It indeed lilted like no other, and I did recall having heard it. Margaret followed most of the words, but her voice swelled with the chorus:

'Wien, Wien, nur du allein
Sollst stets die Stadt meiner Träume sein ...

'It's the sort of song the Vienna Tourist Bureau loves – "Vienna, you alone will always be the city of my dreams." And if you've ever been there, you'll know Viennese dreams are expensive.'
Another city she has visited.
'Tell me about Vienna.'
'Oh, I don't know it well. I was only there for a conference, and when it was over I got a room in a pension for a few extra days. Once you've paid the airfare, it seems silly not to spend a bit more to get to know a place better. Vienna's sort of like Montreal, only more so – a museum to its own past glories. A lot of what they call palaces in heavy baroque style, Karntnerstrasse for delicious but expensive

« 93 »

shopping, and coffee shops where pudgy matrons in suspicious blonde hair nibble cream-filled pastries and screw up their eyes with delight. The Ringstrasse, the Hofburg, surely the ugliest palace I've ever seen, but also the Staatsoper and the Museums. The Kunsthistorisches is worth it for the Brueghels alone – all those pictures of the months, *Hunters in the Snow*, *The Fall of Icarus*, and so on. And that lovely Vermeer of the artist and his model, though it could use a cleaning.'

'No pubs?'

'You're being naughty. The conference organized an evening in Grinzing at a heuriger wine bar. It was very touristy, of course, but the young wine was pleasant as long as you were careful with it, and they had a trio doing Schrammel music.'

'Which is …'

She ran her finger down the CD rack, selected one, replaced the operetta which had just finished. Clarinet, guitar and violin – lively enjoyable music. I could see why it would be popular as background music in a bar. Margaret talked about its origins – the nineteenth-century brothers named Schrammel – its humble suburban status in contrast to the downtown big band music of the Strauss family; she explained about wine bars, the peculiar rules – something about a fresh evergreen bough over the door …

As she talked, I reflected that although she must be about my age, she seems immeasurably more mature. I felt intimidated.

Perhaps she noticed my attention drifting.

'Come dance this last one with me,' she said with her warmest smile, 'and then good night.'

It was a waltz again, and again she moved lightly in my arms, and I thought that if what I felt was love, it was very pleasant.

When the piece ended, Margaret became all chipper efficiency again – taking the cups to the kitchen, getting my coat, shaking the water from my boots onto the slush mat.

'There,' she said as she opened the door, 'both of us reasonably sober and heading to bed reasonably early – how virtuous we are.'

She was making it clear.

'Margaret, it's okay, I don't mind. I didn't assume … I wouldn't presume. Did I get them right – assume and presume?'

'Yes.'

'So good night then, thanks for the lovely evening, thanks for the coffee, and thanks for the beginnings of my musical education.'

'Thank you for the lovely meal – it was very thoughtful.'

We kissed briefly, she hugged me for a long moment, then looked into my eyes: 'Not now ... sometime ... perhaps ... I promise I'll explain.'

'You needn't explain anything, Margaret. I like you as you are, I like us as we are. It was a pleasant evening. I ... enjoy being with you.'

She smiled, kissed me lightly, gaily.

'Margaret, you call me the next time you want to give me a lesson – music, cookery, Montreal nightlife – but not school policy.'

'I'll do that.'

She closed the door.

As I walked down the stairs, I wondered again if I was in love.

I rather fear I am.

Fourteen

'But is she very ill?' I asked …

'I guess she is; yet she looks bravely,' replied the girl, 'and she talks as if she thought of living to see it grow a man.'

She beat Hareton, or any child, at a good, passionate fit of crying.

I entreated, and finally attempted to force her to retire. But I soon found her delirious strength much surpassed mine (she was delirious, I became convinced by her subsequent actions and ravings).

I have learned that being *in love with* (or at least *in like with*) Margaret and being *with* Margaret are two very different things. She is reclusive.

Telephones, for example.

My apartment has a simple ugly pink phone which Ms Felsen obviously banished from her sight. When it rings, I answer it, and when I'm not here the caller gets the Radio Shack answering machine I bought with my parents' Christmas money.

Margaret is high tech. In her living room, she has a telephone with a screen which displays the names and numbers of people calling, and can list the people who have called. It also stores several hundred names and their numbers. She has a wall phone in the kitchen and a portable phone in the bedroom. These home phones have an answering service. In her purse she carries a cellphone with a separate answering service.

But despite all this telecommunications sophistication, she almost never answers any of the phones. And so far as I can tell, she rarely telephones out. Certainly she rarely telephones me, despite '… and I'll get back to you. *Beep.*'

After that last evening, I waited four days before leaving a message to suggest getting together, '… if you're free on the weekend, say, but no big deal …'

She didn't call back for two days, and then only to say she was busy Friday and Saturday, but perhaps Sunday or Monday.

'I'll call if I'm free,' she promised.

But she didn't call.

I waited a few days and tried again with roughly the same result.

I felt like Bridget Jones.

Then Margaret stopped by my office to suggest an excursion to Duluth Street that evening.

'Duluth Street?'

'Duluth, Prince Arthur, streets filled with restaurants where you bring your own wine. Greek, Italian, Portuguese, Thai, some French.'

'I'll bring the wine.'

'No, I'll bring the wine,' she insisted, with amusement in her voice.

We had a pleasant and inexpensive meal, then stopped at a bar for a few drinks on the way home. Lots of bright chatter, lots of sincere chatter, even some affectionate chatter. But this time she didn't invite me in, apologizing that she wanted to get to sleep because she had work do the next morning before class. I thought of my own classes and kissed her a light good night.

In her *Diary*, Bridget Jones insists that men ought to send every woman they know cards, chocolates, roses, diamonds, limousines for Valentine's Day. I'm not at all sure how this applies to me and Margaret. She may be romantic in her preference for Viennese waltzes, but she seems entirely unsentimental in the decoration of her apartment. I decided to ask Harrison.

'When in doubt, send a card.'

'Something more than that!'

'When in hopeless doubt, tape it to a bottle of champagne. Brut for preference.'

'Not chocolates?'

'Fattening.'

'Roses?'

'Megs is not keen on flowers – they only last three days.'

'Champagne lasts an hour.'

'But what an hour!'

On the morning of the day, I brought the gift to the college. Margaret's officemate, Melanie Hippo, was genuflecting before a muffin. As I put the bag on Margaret's chair, Ms Hippo tore herself from her totem:

'One word – *kegelling!*'

I took the brochure and escaped. I was at home correcting essays when Margaret telephoned.

'That was really sweet, Will. And entirely unnecessary. I owe you a dinner – Saturday?'

'Love to.'

'About seven?'

'See you then. No, wait. Margaret, the dictionary doesn't have *kegelling* and Melanie's brochure is a bit opaque ...'

'Pubococcygeus exercises.'

'What?'

'Try Google.'

I again took the precaution of asking Harrison's advice on what to take along to Margaret's dinner.

He noted down three wines.

'Any one will do. You'll know it's a hit if she actually serves it,' he cautioned.

I bought an Australian Cabernet Sauvignon-Shiraz blend for half again as much the Shiraz she prefers and twice what I'd normally spend.

'It will be perfect for the main course,' she looked at her watch, 'in an hour.'

A good start.

I soon realized that Margaret had been more than polite about the meal I cooked her. She served:

• Hors d'oeuvres: smoked salmon on brown bread triangles garnished with red onion, capers, and parsley. Champagne.

• Soup: a Mediterranean soup, more delicate than the one

Harrison served at Christmas, of mixed seafood including octopus, squid, and cuttlefish in a broth flavoured with anise and saffron and 'all the usual stuff'. Muscadet sur lie.

• Main course: herbed rack of lamb, grilled and served with a rich brown sauce and watercress garnish; golden sautéed potato balls; a strange, pleasantly bitter vegetable called Belgian endive sautéed and then grilled with Parmesan cheese. The Cabernet Sauvignon-Shiraz.

• Salad: a light salad of mixed greens (including a red one called radicchio; I've seen the mix in the supermarket) with Margaret's vinaigrette, but different – 'Oh, just the house dressing with balsamic vinegar added.' The remainder of the Muscadet.

• Dessert: she was prepared to make crêpes with mixed berries, but we agreed we were neither of us hungry.

• Afters: café pression and a choice of digestifs – Grand Marnier for me and armagnac for Margaret.

• Music: jazz piano – 'Oscar Peterson, because this *is* Montreal.'

• After that: stunned, overwhelmed guest searching in vain for satisfactory words of gratitude; dismissive shrugs by hostess: 'You're in Montreal, after all ... none of it was very difficult ... it just takes practice ...'

• Throughout: amusing, increasingly animated and affectionate chatter and laughter, quiet moments with warm eyes meeting over rims of glasses, and tentative but increasingly warm linking of fingers across the linen.

• Conclusion: Pleasantly sozzled guest departs by twelve-thirty after affectionate kisses, long, tight hugs, promises to get together soonest, and staggers home, increasingly befuddled by steep Westmount streets.

Since that night little has changed. With the school work piling up, both of us are busy most evenings and weekends. I have a morning schedule this term – eight o'clocks and tens again, and Margaret has afternoons. Through the rest of February and into March, we ate once at my place, once at hers, and once on Duluth Street. Then Harrison insisted we join him for a performance of *The Gondoliers* by the McGill Savoyards in mid-March. He claims he attended five performances. He was ecstatic, and Margaret and I both enjoyed ourselves.

'And as you've enjoyed this one, you'll want to see the Montreal West production of *The Pirates of Penzance* in May. I'll order the tickets.'

'Will?'

'Sure, if you're interested.'

'Order away Harrison, love, order away.'

Our time together is always pleasant, and increasingly affectionate, but not more. She sometimes invites me in afterwards for a coffee or a nightcap, but the goodnight kiss an hour later is restrained.

I am not annoyed or frustrated that we have not become lovers, but as we are both in our thirties, I wonder why we have not. I have to think she is cautious about me, cautious about – what? – the intensity, the anguish, the sweat of … not an affair, but an involvement. (Isn't there a simple, earthy word for *affair*?) And although I am attracted to her, like her, even love her, feel I want to be with her, liked, loved by her, I am beginning to accept that it may go nowhere.

I suppose she has to work out something to do with Harrison. I think I can handle that.

Today, as if to confirm my supposition, Harrison closed the office door when he arrived in the office.

'In recognition of your many kind attentions to the Black Orchid, you have earned a promotion, Captain Ass.'

'I am honoured.'

'But may I essay a personal question?'

'You may; I may not answer it.'

'Have you got Dr Taylor sewed up yet?'

'Very funny. No, we've been out together a few times, but she doesn't want to get involved just now.'

'You aren't smouldering with lust for her delectable bod?'

'She's certainly attractive, but … I don't know – perhaps in time, but I'm not pushing it.'

'Wise of you. And you're not smouldering with lust for the return of Miss Lava Flow?'

'The last I had was a brief e-mail before Christmas; just chit-chat. I gather she'll be back next fall.'

'But the two of you are not an item?'

'I couldn't afford the insurance. Frankly, I think she wants to marry an Icelander, a Viking warrior with the sagas in his blood.'

'You're probably right.'

'If I may reciprocate, Harrison – how are things between you and Margaret?'

'Touché. Well, she turned down both marriage proposals I made her last fall.'

'I should have known better than ask you a serious question.'

'You're in danger of losing your promotion – I did give you a serious answer.'

'You proposed to Margaret?'

'Oh yes, have done regularly since wife four-and-a-half decamped. I try to do it on quarter days.'

'You're not serious.'

'I prefer Old Quarter Days – with Lady Day on April sixth, Midsummer Day on July sixth, Michaelmas on October sixth, and Christmas Day on January sixth. I recommend you try her on New Quarter Days – same names but earlier, as I'm sure you know. Get the jump on me by a few days. Or you could try her on Scottish Quarter Days – I don't recall them off-hand, but Candlemas and Lammas are two of them. You could look it up.'

'She would refuse me.'

'Are you quite sure about that? She has made it clear that I am out of the running, no matter how many times I propose, so you seem a likely candidate. Anyway, repeated proposals flatter a woman, and it's never wrong to flatter a woman.'

'I've always tried to stick close to the truth.'

'An appalling error, especially in Quebec. No, always lie about a woman's age, weight, and appearance. Offer to marry Megs on her twenty-first birthday. If you bump into a woman who's seven months pregnant, you compliment her on the obvious success of her slimming regime. If you don't recognize a woman because she hasn't washed in three days, has just spent six hours mucking out the furnace, and is wearing her husband's third best bowling jacket, you excuse yourself by saying you didn't expect to meet Meg Ryan in your supermarket. Really, Captain Ass, you're so naive, so disingenuous I wonder you've managed to survive.'

As if to confirm Harrison's repeated claim, this evening brought another crisis on the theme of 'things in Quebec are not what they seem.'

I was climbing the last block to the house when I heard the scream. In the light from streetlights and houses, I could make out Marie-Claire prancing to her limousine, and Heidi gesticulating from the front steps. I prudently decided not to cross at once – despite the patches of snow and ice, the limousine sped down the street. Heidi gazed dejectedly after it as I approached.

What now?

'Will? Oh God, come in and have a drink, I need a shoulder to cry on.'

'Of course, Heidi,' I said, not entirely sure my shoulder could take it.

'Just drop your …' waving vaguely at the slush mat, the hooks. 'I don't know if I can … bouleverséed … my world has just been … G&T?'

She indeed put her head on my shoulder and began to sob.

'Bouleverséed. Oh God, what's going to happen to me?'

The words disappeared in sobs. I comforted her until at last she stood back and fixed her eyes on mine. I was reminded of a movie close-up, her focus flitting back and forth from left to right.

'Can I trust you?'

'Yes, Heidi, you can trust me.'

'Will, babe, you're a mensch!'

Abruptly she pressed her lips to mine in a long, fierce kiss. Just as abruptly, she released me and strode along the hall. I reflected that although she was a bit overblown for my taste, she was nonetheless a remarkably voluptuous woman in her red cocktail dress, black stockings and high heels.

I expected to sit in the dining room as usual – close to the bar – but she led me to the living room where we sat before the blazing fire.

'Chin-chin,' she said.

'Cheers,' I replied.

'Ahh, the mean man is tormenting us, Tinker Bell.'

She lifted the dog and cuddled it to her cheek.

'I meant to comfort you. Not very successfully, it seems.'

She took a long swallow of her drink, then surprised me by opening a silver box and taking out a cigarette.

'Do you mind?'

'It's your house, Heidi.'

'I don't smoke around school, and I've been off them since the operations, but I need one now, I really need one ...'

Tinker Bell evidently disapproves of second-hand smoke, for she yipped and ran off. Heidi took a long, thoughtful drag, contemplated the stream of smoke, then burst into tears again.

'Oh hell, my mascara,' she said. 'That's the thing about becoming a woman instead of growing into it – you have so much to learn so quickly. You're a woman so you're allowed to cry, but if you cry your face looks like the roofers have spilled the tar pot. Or fingernails. I used to think that women are vain because they fuss so about filing their nails. Well, you try pulling on your pantyhose and you'll soon understand why women want smooth nails. With day-wear pantyhose at three, four bucks a pop and dress sheers seven and up, you can blow a fortune if your nails have a snag.'

'I have to admit I'd never considered that.'

'Look at these,' she said, pulling her skirt up past the lacy stocking tops. 'Dims stay-ups. I got a dozen pair on sale at The Bay and was lucky to get change from ... oh, hell, I can't remember.'

She butted her cigarette.

'But you aren't interested in the price of stockings.'

'If you think it'll help to talk about the price of stockings, I'll listen. Your relations with Marie-Claire are none of my business, though I'll listen to that too. She's leaving you?'

'She's betraying me.'

'She's found another woman?'

She lit another cigarette.

'No.'

'A man?'

'I wish it was that simple, then I could call her a slut and be done with her. No, Marie-Claire has always been bisexual, like any sensible woman in Quebec, any sensible woman anywhere. Well, I'd prefer that they be exclusively lesbian, obviously, but the joie de vivre of Quebec swings both ways. Marie-Claire has had male lovers, but only if they were French. Her female lovers could be French or English. See, standard male-female sex by definition implies domination by the male – I mean, the very act of penetration is at the least a symbolic act of domination. As a nationalist, Marie-Claire absolutely could not bear domination by an Anglo male – it would be a betrayal of her very soul.'

'A betrayal of the soul of the nation.'

'L'âme de la nation, exactly! Though it's now called the Ministère du sang sacré du peuple.'

She finished her drink; I got her another. When I returned, her black eyes were fixed on the flames.

'Now, when Marie-Claire and I first met, I'd begun the hormone treatments, but I hadn't had the operations. We were attracted to one another at once. Yet, for the first time in my life, I didn't feel I had to penetrate, to dominate – it was the strangest thing. 'If you were completely a woman, Hymie,' she said, 'then I could love you.' Impulsively I replied, 'My tits are already bigger than yours, babe – wait till you see them in a year!' It was a joke; we laughed and laughed. We laughed endlessly in those days. Oh well ...'

She looked thoughtfully at her drink.

'My wife was gone, and I was getting tired of tom-catting around. And with Marie-Claire it was different, there was real communication. She's highly intelligent, she's packed a tremendous amount of living into her forty years, she knows everybody – the President of France, Bill Clinton – hell, she's even met the Pope! Although she didn't nail him.'

'Which means she nailed Clinton and Chirac?'

'And I could tell you a few things about Hillary.'

'Surely Clinton is an Anglo?'

'Yes, but he's a Yank – she only hates Anglo-Canadian men. Anyway, she prefers women and everything feminine, and so do I. I've always loved lingerie, black lace, stockings, elegant high heels, the swish of skirts, and Marie-Claire is *always* feminine, even when she's with another woman.'

As she spoke, she stroked her stockinged thigh.

'So the operation seemed to me a real commitment, not just to my adoration of everything feminine, but to Quebec, to the adjustment of relations between French and English in Quebec. It was not just the natural choice, it was the only choice. And don't you dare say, "Politics makes strange bed-fellows".'

'It hadn't occurred to me,' I lied. 'But Marie-Claire has betrayed your commitment?'

'Not yet, but she wants to. See, Quebec is a world leader in transgender operations. You can add breasts and hips with hormones. Changing male genitalia to female is the classic operation, and they're really good at it now. I mean, if I showed you, you wouldn't know the difference?'

'No, no, that's all right, I'll believe you.'

She gave me a coquettish smile.

'Relax, babe, I'm not interested in men.'

And she burst into tears again.

When I calmed her down she murmured, 'Not interested in men.'

'So what's the problem?'

'Well, I said the male to female procedure is just about perfect, at least for sex – menstruation and pregnancy are still a long way off, of course. But female to male operations have not been nearly so satisfactory. Recently, however, they've been working on transplants, and they've been getting closer and closer.

'As I said, Quebec is at the cutting edge – sorry – of trans-gender operations, and Marie-Claire, as Ministre de le sang sacré du peuple, hears about all the latest achievements long before the word gets out.'

'And ...'

Had I guessed where this was leading?

'And she learned a few days ago that a leading surgeon – not the one who did me, but a colleague – has successfully transplanted male genitalia. Not just the construction of something that looks like it, but an actual transplant, majogglers and all. Of course, they have to wait to see how functional it is, whether the nerves and blood vessels allow erection, whether ejaculation is possible, etc., etc., but so far the operation has been a total success.'

'You mean Marie-Claire wants to have this new operation?'

'Exactly. Well, think about it. She abhors domination by Anglo men – and for some years has refused domination by French men. Becoming lesbian is only half the answer, so now she is going to take the logic to its conclusion – she's going to become a man.'

Somehow it was inevitable.

'Well … uh …' desperate for a response, 'you'll make an … unorthodox couple.'

Her black eyes flashed.

'No, no, I mean, you must be four or five inches taller than Marie-Claire. Of course, the idea that the man should be taller is just custom, but …'

'My God, after what I've just explained – it's as if I told you World War Three was starting and you told me I had dandruff?'

'Sorry. It was very stupid of me.'

'Anyway, we won't be a couple – when she becomes a man she's going to be gay, then she can literally bugger the Anglos.'

'I'll get you another drink.'

Heidi passed out three hours later. Carrying her to her bed was obviously out of the question. I lifted her legs onto the chesterfield and slipped a pillow under her head. The house was warm, so an afghan from one of the chairs would be covering enough. I turned off the fireplace and all but the hall light and let myself out.

Fifteen

I could not half tell what an infernal house we had.

For himself, he grew desperate; his sorrow was of that kind that will not lament. He neither wept nor prayed – he cursed and defied – execrated God and man, and gave himself up to reckless dissipation.

But at home she had small inclination to practise politeness that would only be laughed at, and restrain an unruly nature when it would bring her neither credit nor praise.

As I left for school the next morning, a burly man in a car in front of the house rolled down his window and barked something at me in French.

What now?

'Je n'comprends pas.'

He motioned me over and flashed some sort of ID so quickly I could not read it and muttered something so guttural that I could not understand it. Several electronic devices were attached to the dash. The woman in the driver's seat scowled from behind her clip-board.

'I'm sorry,' I said, 'but mon français laisse à désirer.'

For incompetent Anglos, the phrase next in importance to 'Vous vous avez tromper de numéro.'

He said something which was evidently a curse.

'Where is she?' he demanded.

'Where is who?' I asked.

'You want to make jokes? Me, I'm making the jokes, but you not be laughing. Where is the Felsen broad?'

'I don't know. In the house, at work. I just rent the basement apartment.'

'When you seen her last?'

« 109 »

'Last evening. She invited me in for a few drinks.'

'What time you leaving?'

'About ten, ten-thirty. Look, what's this all about?'

'None of your goddamn business, sacrement, just answer the questions or you gonna be in big trouble. Ten-thirty? Her, she maybe go out then?'

'I don't think so. She was asleep.'

He muttered something.

'Go on, get out of here, you. And you gonna keep your mouth shut, you ain't seen nothing, hunnerstan?'

His window closed smoothly.

Seen nothing? How could I ignore a parked car with its engine running? I might pretend, but around here people report any unfamiliar car within half an hour. Brian Mulroney lives a few blocks away and Heidi says that even before September eleventh, everyone kept watch against irate taxpayers, downsized civil servants, and unsuccessful place-seekers. In any case, no one could miss the succession of unmarked cars which replaced one another in a round-the-clock vigil, but always in the same place, always with two people inside, always with the engine running to keep the heater on.

At school, Tracy told me Heidi had called in sick. The next day she was still off, with the watchers in front producing in the snow a growing fan of coffee cups and doughnut boxes.

I was worried about Heidi, so I consulted Harrison.

'Ahh, the Sûreté du Québec, the doughnut dragoons who guard the peace and security of every Québécois and Québécoise. Except the innocent. Especially if they lay carpets – don't ask. Poor Little Buttercup, it's a betrayal. And of course Marie-Claire, as a good little Cartesian, is only carrying it out to the logical end. But I expect we must help Heidi. Are you sure she's still able to fog a mirror?'

'She doesn't answer the doorbell or the phone, but her newspapers are on the porch every morning and they're gone later. I've looked through the door and she must be picking her mail off the floor.'

'As I recall, you can get from your apartment to Heidi's part of the house.'

'She usually locks the door at the top of her stairs.'

'I expect we can manage something. In the meantime, you'll be interested to hear that Miss Viking Scourge is being flown in to take Ms Felsen's classes for the rest of the term.'

'Ahh ...'

'I expect it will also interest Dr Taylor.'

'Interest her? Upset her, more likely. Why does Margaret dislike Gudrun?'

'No idea. I'd better get some booze for Heidi. Drop by my house on your way home and I'll drive you up.'

Margaret was indeed upset. She stormed into the office an hour later and shut the door.

'Where the hell is Harrison?'

'He went home.'

'Have you heard the news?'

'About Heidi? Yes.'

'No, they're flying Gudrun home, for God's sake.'

'Doesn't she get cheap flights or something because her father works for an airline?'

'You know that's not what I'm talking about! In two weeks, we'll be telling ourselves Heidi is lucky to be out of here – if we're all still speaking to one another.'

'I'll still be speaking to you, Margaret.'

'Don't bet on it – she's already sampled the goods, and no doubt she'll want more.'

'Come on, Margaret, I told you she left her bag in my place, but she slept upstairs.' Well, no, I was not telling the whole truth. 'I doubt she lies awake thinking of me. I certainly don't lie awake thinking of her.'

Margaret glared at me a long moment; then her whole body relaxed.

'Sorry,' she said. 'I shouldn't have said anything. Are you busy?'

I shrugged, waved at the essays on my desk. 'My chairs at home aren't as comfortable as this one.'

She rolled Harrison's chair over to my desk and sat.

'Did you mean that? About not thinking about her?'

'Yes.'

Whatever the past, it was the truth.

She shook her head, sought the words.

'Will, I'm ... frightened.'

I was stunned. The notion of Margaret frightened of anything was incongruous, absurd.

'Of Gudrun?'

'No. Yes. Frightened of Gudrun, of you, of me.'

'You needn't be frightened of Gudrun. Just keep her away from the china. Don't let her play with matches.'

Margaret gazed at me.

'And you needn't be frightened of me – I'm just an ordinary guy. A baguette.'

She kissed me lightly on the forehead and was gone.

To avoid the SQ, we parked on the next street and made our way through the back yards.

Inside, after a glance about, Harrison declaimed:

> 'Far away from toil and care,
> Revelling in mountain air,
> Here you live and reign alone
> In a world that's all your own.

'Now, how to get to Mlle Mésalliance?'

I led him though into the basement proper and we tiptoed up the stairs.

'The door is serious, but the lock is a joke. I was worried it might have a Yale or a dead bolt. Got a bobby-pin?'

'That's more Heidi's sort of accessory than mine.'

'There must be a work room or something down here – show me.'

He used pliers to cut a short length of coat-hanger and to bend an angle at one end. In ten seconds he unlocked the door and we were in Heidi's hallway.

The newspapers and the mail lay on the floor by an overturned chair. Several paintings were askew, and a half eaten sandwich lay in the living room doorway beside an empty wine bottle.

'Say, why is everything either at sixes or at sevens?' murmured Harrison.

He craned forward to survey the living room, then back toward the dining room and kitchen.

Suddenly Heidi's voice called out from above:

'Who the hell is skulking about down there? I warn you, I've got a vicious pit bull up here. And, if it's the goddamn SQ, there's not a doughnut in the house, pas de beignes, cawliss, so piss off.'

'Relax, Heidi, and chain up the killer beast, it's me and Major Ass.' He added in a whisper, 'This exploit earns you a promotion.'

'Superstud to the rescue, eh? Get out or I'll have your balls for bookends – and around here, fella, that's no joke.'

'Well, since we've taken the trouble to drop by, the least you can do is offer us a drink. What kind of hospitality have you got on display here?'

We heard her feet on the stairs.

'Hell, if you can find a drink you're welcome to it. Let's take a look in the bar. Did you at least bring the customary bottle of wine? I don't have any obligation to cheapskates.'

'What the hell, Heidi, you look like a floozie – you planning to open a brothel?'

Heidi's black silk robe was open to reveal her black bustier, and her legs were encased in the same black stockings she'd been so proud of when I last saw her.

'Gimme a break, Harrison, I'm practising coming downstairs in high heels. How's this for an elegant walk, eh?'

'Eat your heart out, Claudia Schiffer,' Harrison replied. 'And we aren't cheapskates.'

'Scotch! Oh, thanks a lot, Harrison, you selfish son of a bitch – I finished my gin yesterday and now you offer me this Gaelic piss. Shit. Well, what are we waiting for, get some glasses and I'll turn on the fireplace.'

'Well, dear lady, what do you plan to do about the beigne brigade?'

'We could shoot them,' said Heidi.

'A policeman's lot is not a happy one.'

'But I don't have a gun.'

'Usually considered an essential.'

'Okay, how about baking them a batch of poisoned doughnuts?'

'Great idea – got any poison? Mouse bait? Ant poison?'

'Naw, the only vermin around this place is young Will here.'

'Set Tinker Bell on them.'

'Knowing the SQ, they'd probably whip a barbecue out of the trunk and eat her.'

'That's rather what I was hoping.'

'You're not helping. Hm ... sword ... spear ... crossbow ...'

'I gnashed my teeth, when from its sheath I drew my snickersnee. No, something more modern, Heidi.'

'Hey, we could put a bomb under their car. Rumour has it you can make bombs from ingredients found in every household.'

'Get online, Major Ass, and if you find us a practical recipe I'll promote you to lieutenant colonel.'

'I thought you just wanted them to go away, not go away forever.'

'Piss off, kid.'

'Naw, the major's got a point, Heidi.'

'The top of his head. Wait a minute – they leave their engine running all the time to keep the heater going.'

'So?'

'So it's a Westmount bylaw that you can't run your engine for more than ten minutes while you're parked.'

'We don't live in Westmount any more, Heidi.'

'Shit, I told Marie-Claire the municipal mergers were a lousy idea, but she said the cabinet was determined to screw the Anglos.'

'Besides, the cruller commandos are above the law.'

'Especially when dealing with Anglos – and what worse, I'm Jewish.'

'Heidi, don't bother the major with all that rococo lunacy – two solitudes, language laws, separatism, antisemitism, and all that – no one gives a damn about it any more. Anyway, he's having enough trouble staying mad as it is.'

Heidi shook her head, and stroked my arm. 'How do you put up with this sumbitch officemate, anyway?'

'Because the kid is semi-crazy.'

Heidi at once got to her feet and draped herself over Harrison's shoulders.

'That's why I love this sumbitch – he's so goddam sharp – he got the reference right off.'

'I'm afraid I ...'

'A novel, a movie called *Semi-Tough*. Before your time. A real scholar, a semi-genius, isn't he, Tinks.'

Tinker Bell yipped admiringly at Harrison.

'Heidi, lose the rug rat, we're not getting any closer to a solution. And you've stolen the bottle again.'

I wanted to get away, but thought I ought to suggest a harmless plan before they got so drunk they'd do something dangerous.

'Excuse me, but do we actually know why the SQ are out there?'

The consensus was that they were to forestall Heidi from harassing Marie-Claire.

'Well,' I continued, 'what if we convince them that Heidi has lost interest in Marie-Claire?'

'Convince the SQ?' cried Heidi. 'You'd have to be semi-brilliant to convince those mouth-breathers that two and two are four!'

'Hang on, Heidi. What were you suggesting, Major?'

'Well, what if they think she's in love with one of us?'

'But how?'

'Well, we could go in the living room and ... I don't know, make it obvious that we're having a party, that Heidi's whooping it up without help from Marie-Claire.'

'Have some Scotch, Major – I think you're on to something.'

'Hey, you're giving him the last of the bottle!'

'We've got three more.'

'That's what I mean, we only have three more.'

'But,' I said carefully, 'I think you should be sober enough to dance.'

Harrison understood.

'I believe Major Ass is suggesting we put on a show at the front window – if they see you slow dancing, locked in a passionate embrace with him, they'll report ...'

'Now wait just a semi-minute here – I don't want Marie-Claire thinking I'm getting it on with Will. She's seen him, so she knows he's a semi-hunk. She'd go bananas.'

'Once more into the breach, dear friends,' Harrison intoned. 'If *breach* is indeed the word I'm looking for here.'

'Hey, you want to see my breach?'

'No.'

'At least look at the boobs!'

Before we could object, she had pulled down the cups of her bustier and tucked them under her breasts. Harrison whistled.

'Magnificent hooters, babe. Didn't think you had them in you.'

'Every man has them in him – he just needs enough of the hormones. What about the rings? Nifty, eh? They were Christmas presents from ... from Marie-Claire.'

Five minutes sufficed to end the sobs.

'But, snuffle, sniff, we really want you to see the pièce de résistance, don't we, Tinker Bell.'

'Perhaps later. In the meantime, shall we dance?'

Heidi put on a Frank Sinatra CD of slow ballads. While they danced in close embrace before the window, I crept into the front hall to see if the SQ were reacting.

At first, I thought they were asleep, but then the near one took a bite of a doughnut. However, they weren't looking at the house. I reported to the others.

'Put on some Stones,' said Harrison, 'crank up the volume, and turn on the light over there.'

When I next peeked out, both SQ officers were gazing in.

'Got 'em,' I reported.

Heidi stopped dancing and gave Harrison a long passionate kiss.

'Bring the bottle,' Harrison hissed when his mouth was free.

Heidi's breasts were still exposed; as she leaned against the window frame and held up her glass for Harrison to pour, she presented her profile to the surveillance, so that her dark nipples with the glinting rings were well lit and no doubt clearly visible from outside.

'Hey, babe, how about kissing the nips – that'll semi-freak them out?'

I didn't see if Harrison kissed them or not, because I was in the vestibule, but I did see that the officer in the passenger seat was talking into a radio or cellphone handset.

'Bingo,' I reported.

'Bingo?' Harrison complained. 'Is *bingo* the best you can do?'

'How about, 'He shoots, he scores'?'

'That's not only inept, it's Toronto.'

'Touché?'

'Stale, but it'll have to do. Where's the Grouse?'

Ten minutes later I was able to report that the SQ were driving away. We retired to the dining room to celebrate our victory.

With more Scotch.

'To our cute semi-young colleague – a semi-genius!'

'To Lieutenant Colonel Ass, on his second promotion of the day.'

I bowed in humility.

'But it's only the opening skirmish,' said Heidi. 'Now we've got to get Marie-Claire to calm down and reconsider.'

'I explained to you,' Harrison sighed, 'we'll get Gudrun to do it.'

'I'm not convinced. She'll end up burning down my house ... or the ministry.'

'Trust me.'

'Men keep saying that to me, but I was a man for long enough to know what a bunch of lying twisters you all are.'

'Gudrun's not a man. Pass the bottle.'

'Here. And a reward for you, Will, you sweetie. You've seen my bazooms, time to look at, as promised, the pièce de résistance!'

Before I could object, Heidi stood up and pushed her panties down to her knees, thrusting her pelvis forward.

'*Pièce* is the right word, babe,' said Harrison. 'Come to think of it, I could go for some fur pie about now.'

'Piss off, Harrison, this is dessert – it goes with lady fingers, not bratwurst.'

My brief glance suggested it was entirely convincing.

'Well, uh, look, I have a morning class, and ...'

'Sumbitch!' cried Heidi.

'Wanker!'

'Loser!'

'Upper Canadian!'

'I'm a Nova Scotian.'

'Bluenoser!'

'Brown-noser!'

I managed it within five minutes. As I paused at the door, Heidi was sitting on the corner of the dining room table and pointing down as Harrison leaned forward.

'... see, to make this little nubbins here, they cut a bit from my ...'

I stayed awake only long enough to set my alarm, so missed the SQ raid sometime after 5 a.m.

❧

Sixteen

Then personal appearance sympathised with mental deterioration.

'Then they what?' cried Catherine, gazing at him with a troubled countenance.

He entered, vociferating oaths dreadful to hear.

'But I don't like the carving knife, Mr Hindley,' I answered; 'it has been cutting red herrings. I'd rather be shot, if you please.'

I spat out, and affirmed it tasted detestably – I would not take it on any account.

'No, you forget, Mrs Linton,' I suggested, 'that you have eaten some food with a relish this evening, and tomorrow you will perceive its good effects.'

'What a noise for nothing!' I cried, though rather uneasy myself.

The drama of Gudrun's arrival surprised no one. Late for her first class, she was running up the stairs when she encountered Tabitha Hippo doing something profane to a muffin. Gudrun embraced her, gushed her joy at being back, and rushed through the door into our corridor. Tabitha turned to call, 'One word – *Robertson Davies collectibles!*' and tripped. Departmental wisdom has it that hip replacement is as easy as getting a tooth filled these days, but Tabitha will not be chairing the gender equality committee anytime soon.

Unaware of this disaster, Gudrun stopped by the department office. Within seconds Tracy's screen went blank, then a crude cartoon man in an overcoat flashed her and informed her that her hard drive was being formatted as a protest against 'global warmming, eat meat, thong panties, and zoning regoulation impositioned by recidivist city counseil of Vilnius Lithuania.'

No one claims that Gudrun caused the virus, the failures of three department marriages, the Jewish-Muslim riot, or the flooding of the library, but suspicions persist.

Even before his arrest, Harrison had taken the precaution of hanging a cross above his desk, tying a string of garlic to a filing cabinet drawer, and discreetly daubing lamb's blood on the doorposts and lintel.

I didn't see her at school; however, my encounter with her later in the day was no less dramatic than Tabitha Hippo's.

Although Harrison missed his classes because he was in the slammer, he would have booked off with a hangover anyway. However, he and Heidi were out by early afternoon. As soon as I got home, Heidi yelled down the stairs and invited me up for a celebratory G&T.

'In ten minutes, dearie – we're dying for a shower, aren't we, Tinker Bell? But I'll leave the door open, so just come up and build our drinks when you hear the water stop.'

I was sipping mine and examining her collection of hedgehogs when Heidi descended.

'You like?' she demanded, doing a pirouette.

She was wearing the usual black stockings and high heels, but the dress was one I hadn't seen before, a flouncy red and black cocktail dress with figured bead work on the shoulders and bodice, and a neckline which plunged to her waist. Across her cleavage hung a gold chain.

'I bought the dress and the chain to please Marie-Claire, but if the bitch doesn't want to see them, I've decided to show them off for you and the others.'

She pulled the bodice aside to show that the chain was clipped to her nipple rings.

'You're taking to this with considerable enthusiasm,' I remarked.

'I enjoy being a girl,' she sang. 'But you'll have to excuse me while I use the curling iron – another thing you'll notice when you become a woman is the hours you have to spend doing your hair. Men! You're so lucky!'

'So what was all this legal fuss?'

'Oh, the cowboys threatened to charge me with keeping a common bawdy house and selling alcohol without a licence, and Harrison as a found-in or living off the avails. And both of us with high treason, corrupting the National Assembly, stealing the crown jewels of Quebec – wee Bernie Landry keeps them in his jockstrap – of eating sushi, of thinking we are better than other people, and of being Anglo-imperialist tools of the international Jewish conspiracy. Just the usual shit. Of course, between us we have enough lawyer friends to fight it to the Supreme Court of Canada on good will alone. And the SQ has no jurisdiction in Montreal for most of those charges, so it was just harassment and they finally had to let us go. But the cells! A good thing you weren't there, Tinks, you sensitive soul! You'd have been shocked, wouldn't you, my sweetums, by the riff-raff – drunks, hookers, vagrants, and a bunch of biker girls in leathers from a drug bust in Rosemere or somewhere, too, too butch! And me a nice Jewish girl from Côte St-Luc in nothing but my bustier and housecoat – you can't imagine!'

The doorbell announced the arrival of Harrison and Gudrun, he still hung over and she jet-lagged.

'Hair of the dog, fellow con, or G&T? For you, Gudrun?'

Of course both had to admire Heidi's chain and rings, then glasses were raised and Heidi and Harrison began comparisons of their incarcerations. I was not at all enthusiastic about another night of alcohol abuse, but Heidi insisted I stay at least until she could 'whip up a little Italian nuova cucina, sweetie.' While she and Harrison went to the kitchen, Gudrun and I remained in the dining room. I was pondering a subject of polite conversation when I heard my phone ringing downstairs. It wasn't a wrong number, it was Margaret.

'Sorry, were you just coming in the door?'

'I was upstairs. Heidi got out of jail this afternoon and invited me up.' I thought it best to tell all. 'And Harrison just arrived with Gudrun. I'm still recovering from last night, but after their arrest they want to celebrate. It's a sort of obligation, but I'm leaving as soon as the meal is over.'

'A catered affair, no less.'

'Heidi's doing something with pasta. Listen, if you want to meet in an hour or so …'

She paused, then said, 'I don't think so.'

I could sense the tension in her voice.

'Has something happened? Is it Gudrun?'

'No, it's just that Coretta Toadie was in my office promoting modelling clay as a teaching aid, and I sort of lost it. I shouldn't have bothered you.'

'No bother, Margaret. Listen, give me a call when you're free.'

'Okay.'

Upstairs, Heidi and Harrison were still in the kitchen. Gudrun was at the dining room table reading Beauvoir's *Le deuxième sexe* from the mantelpiece, and with one of the jars of thousand-year eggs open in front of her.

'It's good, try a bite,' she said as she pressed the last of the egg against my lips.

'No thanks.'

I pushed her hand gently away.

'It's supposed to be an egg, but it tastes more like a sausage, but it isn't a sausage. Who was that on the phone?'

'Just some telemarketer – I suppose they have them in Denmark too?'

'Yes, but they do their pitch in Danish and I reply in Icelandic and when they say they can't understand I tell them they're dunces who don't even know their own language.'

'I thought Icelandic was based on West Fjord Norwegian.'

'That's not something your average Danish telemarketer knows.'

She opened the second jar and speared the egg with her fork.

'It could do with some mustard. And some salt and pepper,' and went to the kitchen.

'You want ball park?' I heard Heidi ask. 'Dijon? German? Look in the fridge door, second shelf from the top.'

Indistinct snatches of Heidi and Harrison talking, cutlery and plates clinking.

Gudrun came back with a jar and a spoon. 'This Oktoberfest mustard will be exactly right.' She spooned some onto the egg and took a big bite.

Heidi was saying, 'Now rub the grated Parmesan to ...' but paused then called, 'Gudrun, sweetie, what did you want the mustard for?'

Gudrun finished chewing and said to me, 'Perfect. Go on, take a bite.'

'No thanks.'

'Gudrun?'

'For the sausage,' Gudrun called between chews.

Pause.

'Sausage? What sausage?'

Heidi came running.

'What sausage?'

'You said these were thousand-year eggs, but they taste more like súrsaðir hrútsprungar.' She popped the last morsel into her mouth. 'That's an Icelandic specialty – pickled ram's testicles, so maybe you should call it a thousand-year sausage, no big deal, I mean ...'

She swallowed.

'But it's got a really delicate flavour, I've never tasted anything quite like it before.'

Heidi slumped into a chair and dropped her head onto her arms.

'What?' Gudrun asked. She looked at me, at Harrison standing in the doorway.

Heidi lifted her head and said softly, 'I should bloody well hope you've never tasted it before,' she said, 'you ... you cannibal!'

Only Harrison had the composure to speak.

'Congratulations, Heidi – at a guess, you're the first woman in history who's had her own balls for bookends.'

The next morning Gudrun knocked on the door from the basement and stuck her head in.

'Hi-iii, you're up!'

She was wearing only a T-shirt top and, I assumed, panties.

'Good morning,' I said. 'Coffee?'

'Gosh, have you got it right – in Iceland you always offer coffee as soon as a guest arrives.'

'How are things upstairs?'

'Heidi's still asleep. But what a fuss! I mean, really, if she thought they were so valuable, why did she have them lopped off?'

'I suppose they had sentimental value. Like graduation photos.'

'Or a piece of wedding cake.'

'I am glad I didn't try one. How did you manage to keep them down after you learned?'

'I don't know – I just didn't feel like throwing up. After all, we Icelanders don't just eat súrsaðir hrútsprungar, we eat whale meat, puffin, guillemot and hakarl, that's putrefied shark meat. Anyway,' she leaned forward and whispered, 'they were scrumptious!'

Margaret's summing up of Gudrun echoed ghoulishly – 'She eats men.'

'I'll take your word for it.'

She smacked her lips.

The telephone interrupted an increasingly uncomfortable subject.

'Hello,' I chirped. No response. 'Hello?'

'A telemarketer on Saturday morning?' asked Gudrun.

I hastily hung up, but suspected the sound of Gudrun's voice had done the damage.

'Well,' I said to change the subject, 'did you get around to discussing Heidi's problem with Marie-Claire after I left?'

'Oh, yes, but really, if you men have to become women, the least you could do is learn to think and feel like a woman. I mean, Heidi is totally freaked about her – and I don't see what the problem is – it's not as if Marie-Claire is God's gift to women. Frankly, she's more than a bit of a bitch, and lately she's been going a bit wacko. I mean, I admit she's great in bed, but so are lots of other women, so why put up with her bitchiness when there are so many sweet chicks around?'

'Harrison seems to think you can patch it up.'

'Well, of course I can patch it up. In the *Laxdæla Saga*, Guðrún Osvifsdóttir – who is a super babe, by the way – is married to Þorvald Halldorsson, but she doesn't love him, and she wants to marry Þord Ingunnarsson, but he's already married to a woman named Auðr, so she has to fix two divorces. Guess how she does it.'

I put her coffee on the table.

'Tell me.'

'Well, she makes her husband a shirt with a neck cut so low that his nipples show, and when he wears it, that's grounds for divorce. And Auðr wears breeches and a codpiece, and that's also grounds for divorce.'

'Sounds as if ancient Iceland was a sexually adventurous place.'

'It was – you should read the sagas.'

'And somewhat less tolerant of sexual adventuring than modern Quebec is. But surely you don't plan something like that for Marie-Claire?'

'Oh, of course not, although I do plan on getting her to Iceland. I'm just pointing out that we Guðrúns are experienced in dealing with the many-sexed.'

'But you think you can persuade Marie-Claire not to have the operation?'

'Oh, yes, it's all so silly, because she hates men anyway, so why become one? If she's so keen, she can use a strap-on – these days they make some that are almost as good as the real … Oh, sorry, give me a cloth and I'll wipe it up, but I'm sure the stain will never show on this dark carpet.'

'Never mind, Gudrun, I'll do it.'

As I bent to wipe up the coffee, Gudrun stood up and whacked my ear with her chair.

When she was settled with another coffee, Gudrun said, 'So, I hear you have something going with the Black Death?'

'We're friends.'

I rather resented her use of Harrison's meanest nickname for Margaret and the careful scrutiny Gudrun gave me over the rim of her cup.

'Is that all?'

'We've had a few dates.'

'Good, but try harder, because you're going to marry her – I'm a völva, so I know – but be really careful, because she could break your heart.'

'Because she's still in love with Harrison?'

'Yes,' she replied, but I noticed that she looked away evasively.

'You don't seem convinced your prophecy will come true.'

'Oh, my prophecies always come true – didn't I tell you the college would hire you full-time for next fall?'

'That's true,' I admitted, 'and Heidi says three people are retiring, just as you predicted.'

'Well, there you are.'

'So what do you prophesy for Heidi and Marie-Claire?'

'Oh, they're destined for fame, for immortality – at least in Iceland.'

'Really? How?'

But her eyes were again evasive.

'That's obscured by the veils of time. But it's certain. I mean, they're gender adventurers, they're showing the way and perhaps someday everyone will change their sex at some point. Women would have to wait until they'd had their babies, obviously, but if they changed right after giving birth they wouldn't have postpartum hip spread – no more love handles!'

As usual, I hadn't bothered to lock the door after getting the paper – home invasions aren't common in this part of Westmount. But now the door opened and my home was invaded.

'I came to see if I could help you with Heidi,' said Margaret, 'but you obviously have all the help you need.'

'Gee, Margaret, hi,' said Gudrun, retreating toward the inner door. 'Gosh, I'd love to stay and chat, but I told Heidi I'd only be five minutes … Oops!' She caught her foot on a pile of books and stumbled, revealing to us both that she wasn't wearing panties.

'Bye-eee!'

'Well,' I said in the heavy silence, 'would you like a coffee.'

'You're offering me a coffee?'

In the grubbiness of my apartment, she looked particularly elegant in her black loden coat and matching wide-brimmed hat.

'Well, now that I have the pression maker, I …'

She was staring at my bed, still unmade.

'I'll throw this out and wash the cup – I only have the two cups, but it'll only take …'

'Only one person slept there.'

'Yes, you see …'

'There's no luggage?'

'No, well, Gudrun is staying with Heidi until she gets …'

Margaret slumped onto the bed and covered her face with her

hands. As the sobs grew, she lowered her head to the pillow and lay on her side with her knees drawn up. I sat beside her and stroked her shoulder, her arm, murmuring meaningless reassurances. I felt a hopeless sadness for this lovely woman, usually so strong, so confident. What was frightening her? Surely she didn't care about me enough to be jealous? And why might she love me when she loves the far more interesting and amusing Harrison?

'Perhaps I'll have that coffee now,' she whispered after a few minutes.

While I fiddled about in the kitchenette, she took off her boots and coat and joined me as the water came to the boil. She put her arm around my waist and leaned her head against my shoulder.

As she raised the cup to her lips she shivered slightly.

'Are you cold? I can turn up the heat.'

'Not cold, no.'

I left it to her to explain or not.

At last she asked, 'Have you had many girlfriends, Will?'

I'd never counted.

'Not many. Perhaps eight since I began university.'

'Eight?' incredulously.

'Well, you asked for girlfriends. If you include brief flings I suppose you could double the number.'

'Sixteen women in all? Harrison does that in a year!'

'You told me he doesn't do students, and I've never seen eligible candidates around the office.'

'No, I'll grant him that – and in the one case I know about, he waited at least a year until I graduated.'

'Yes, well …'

Margaret considered. 'On the other hand, he's hell on the discontented wives of Westmount.'

'I'm not Harrison. Besides, I gather most of his conquests were in the seventies – make love, not war – before AIDS. And you and I grew up after it appeared, so no free love for us.'

'No,' softly. 'No free love for us.'

'And I've gradually come to realize that apart from AIDS and the other STDs, I … well, I don't much enjoy going to bed with a woman unless … unless I'd at least consider marrying her. I know that sounds terribly old-fashioned, but it seems to be true.'

'From what I know of you, I can believe it.'

'Anyway, it's just me, a notion.' I looked into her eyes and repeated, 'It's just me – I don't expect it, I don't assume it of others.'

It was probably not necessary, but I wanted her to be sure.

'That seems impossibly generous, impossibly understanding of you.'

'Excuse me while I polish my halo.'

She was studying me with her most piercing stare, her intelligence fully engaged. She looked at her cup, looked up, smiled.

'I have the car – how about croissants?'

She was heartbreakingly appealing.

As we put our on coats I wondered about all we hadn't said.

Seventeen

The return of sunshine was welcomed by answering sunshine from him. I believe I may assert that they were really in possession of deep and growing happiness.

Good night – I'm an angel!

Margaret drove us over the mountain to a chichi place where the croissants and coffee were delectable, and everyone but us was speaking French.

'I've never been in this part of town,' I admitted, leaning confidentially across the table.

'Actually, it's a naughty choice, because this is supposed to Marie-Claire's favourite place for brunch.'

'She doesn't seem to be here now.'

'She's probably in Paris giving the French hell for using too many English words.'

As we walked back to the car, Margaret snuggled against me. I'm beginning to get used to this.

'Well, now, do you have time for some education?'

'No work that I can't put off until tomorrow.'

'In that case, I have a few ideas.' First out to IKEA where she filled our cart with a careful selection of kitchen gadgets, many of which – a whisk, a garlic press, a mortar and pestle – I'd never have thought of buying. Despite the Saturday crowds, we were out of there in an hour. Back downtown to a shop where she made me buy herbs and spices, some of which I had never even heard of before – chervil, saffron, mace, star anise, cumin. I also got black, white, red and green peppercorns and a pack of bottles for storing everything.

'One o'clock. Have you ever had Montreal bagels fresh from the oven?'

'I've had bagels fresh from a plastic bag in Edmonton.'

Margaret sighed.

'I said "bagels", not "tasteless doughy doughnut-shaped things" – come along.'

As we waited in line in the little shop, we watched a man and a woman roll the dough into rings. Another man scooped a batch from a large pot of boiling brownish liquid, dipped some in a bowl of poppy seed, some in sesame seed, laid them on a long plank, then slid the plank into a low, deep wood oven. He used the plank to turn whole lines of half baked bagels on other planks; he removed a plank of finished bagels from the oven and dumped them into a bin. A girl bagged a dozen for us, half poppy seed, half sesame seed.

'Have one while they're hot,' said Margaret as we walked back to the car. 'We'll eat the rest later.'

That bagel was neither the first nor last delight of the day.

She drove up Mount Royal and we walked, strolled, skipped about in the spring sunshine, ate more bagels, surveyed the panorama up and down the river, south to the mountains, to New York and Vermont. Embraced, kissed.

Margaret took her lips from mine and whispered, 'Let me treat you to dinner.'

'It's a bit late for shopping.'

'Ever practical, my dear – no, in a restaurant.'

'But …'

'You paid for the bagels – it's my turn.'

We bargained over wine and tip, but she stood firm on paying for the meal. We separated to shower and change, then strolled down St Catherine Street.

'It's traditional bourgeois French provincial, and it's been here, virtually unchanged, for ages, and has appeared in at least one novel, by … oh, some minor Montreal writer. Perhaps the name will come to me.'

As usual – and as it was all through this marvellous day – this new bit of Montreal was a revelation. I am beginning to see why my friends love this city.

'Do you suppose,' I said as we reached her street, 'that a day like this is the sort of day that defines a happy marriage?'

'Is that a proposal?'

'No. Well ... yes, if you want to take it that way. I only meant it as a way of saying the day was special, unexpected, joyful, yet entirely comfortable – that's the part that seems most like a marriage.'

'I pity the poor woman who'd have to live up to her side of that bargain.'

'Anyway, Harrison keeps telling me I should propose to you, and ...'

'... anything Harrison says ...'

'I've put my foot in it, haven't I?'

We were standing in front of her building before Margaret answered.

'No, you haven't put your foot in it. And you're right – no matter how perverse he sounds, Harrison is often wise.' She looked at me and dropped her voice to a murmur. 'And whether you were surreptitiously proposing or just saying thanks for the day ... thank you for sharing it with me ... for being you.'

She put her arms around me and we kissed, embraced, kissed with passion.

Margaret pulled away.

'I must go. But soon ... we'll get together again soon.'

Harrison started in on me as soon as I got to the office.

'Did she accept?'

'Did who accept what, Harrison?'

'Did the Black Orchid, a.k.a. Megs Taylor, PhD, accept your proposal of marriage?'

'I ...'

Isolde Hippo spread her tent in the doorway.

'No!' we cried.

'One word – *incontinence pads!*'

'No!'

She threw some brochures and waddled off.

'Come along, Lieutenant Colonel Ass –

'The flowers that bloom in the spring,
            Tra la,
    Breathe promise of merry sunshine –

'You could not have spent a whole day arm-in-arming around the chic Plateau, glomming bagels, swanning about Mount Royal, batting eyelashes over gemütlich candle-lit napery without suggesting you make it official. QED. Did she accept?'

'Why didn't you ask her when she told you about it?'

'She wouldn't tell me. I expect you have noticed that Maggie, professionally rational and decisive at work, is stunningly amateurish and indecisive in matters of the heart.'

'She does seem a bit unsure of herself at times.'

Did he know about her married lover?

'Unsure? Terrified, surely?' Harrison insisted.

'Well ...'

'Frightened, at least. Wouldn't you agree that frightened is the word?'

'As it's the word she used when she was talking to me, I have to assume she told you as well. So your question is rhetorical.'

'Don't get pettish, Lieutenant Colonel Ass. Maggie really is frightened, but in the muddled styling of our muddle-headed students, *She has feelings for you.*'

'Loathsome phrase. I don't allow it in essays.'

'Neither do I. We'll whip them into shape yet. So how would you wipe the mud of the muddle from your dealings with Maggie?'

I sighed, pulled the essays from my shoulder bag.

'I don't know. If she wants to be closer to me, I'll know, and if she wants to explain the delay, she will. Margaret is hardly muddled.'

'And what do you suppose is delaying her?'

'I have no idea. And it's none of my business.'

'Of course you have an idea, a clutch of ideas, and of course it's your business. Don't try dumping muddle on me.'

Margaret had likely asked him to quiz me, and my reply would go back to her, so it had to be careful, diplomatic, because even Harrison might muddle nuances.

'Well ... I'm not sure I can put this into words. I can't see it, but I can ... sense something, a sort of presence, looming behind her.'

'You sense it? How sense?'

Was he admitting an *it*?

'I told you, it's vague. Something to do with her phones – she's got home phones and a cellphone, but she almost never answers. On the other hand, why should she? Lots of people don't like answering the phone, and she has answering services.'

'Is that all?'

'Well, she often says she's seeing a friend named Julia, but she never mentions Julia otherwise.'

'And what have you guessed what it might be?'

'Well, I think the most likely explanation is that she is having an affair with a married man, probably someone rich or powerful – a corporate executive, politician, diplomat – someone with a reason for keeping the affair secret. I'm guessing she's trying to break it off, but there are complications.'

'Any candidates?'

'I know nothing about the rich and powerful of Montreal.'

'No one?'

'Well, I live a few blocks from a former prime minister.'

'Muldoon!' Harrison gasped. 'Muldoon?'

'I'm not nominating him, for heaven's sake – I just mentioned him because he's the only rich and powerful Montrealer I know of.'

'No, Muldoon's out of the question – Megs has better taste.'

'Well, Montreal still has a few head offices and consulates that could produce candidates. But then he – if there is a *he* – could live in Toronto or New York or Paris. I don't know, and frankly I don't care. I just hope Margaret is happy. With him or without him, with me or without me.'

'What an admirable man, you are, Lieutenant Colonel Ass.'

'Harrison, I'm hardly admirable – I'm just an ordinary guy trying to get through life without causing too much damage.'

'That's admirable!'

'Put a sock in it.'

'Picking up sock, opening mouth, inserting sock, sir.'

While his teasing irritated me, his concern for Margaret reminded me not to be priggish.

'Harrison, be serious for a moment. How can I help Margaret?'

His levelled eyes told me I could not doubt him.

'Are you willing to love her, believe her, trust her?'

'I think so.'

'Even if she's a heroin dealer? A murderer? An Al-Qa'ida terrorist?'

'Those don't seem very likely possibilities.'

'Even if – horrors! – she's having an affair with a former-prime-minister-who-shall-remain-nameless? Or with Bozo the current PM?'

'Yes.'

'To have and to hold from this day forward, for better for worse, for richer for poorer, in sickness and in health, to love and to cherish, till death do you part, according to God's holy ordinance; and thereto you plight your troth?'

'That sounds as if you have it word for word.'

'I should – I've plighted it often enough. Have you got the nous to do it once? To do it honestly?'

'You're asking me if I'm special, if I'm, what, morally superior? What's the failure rate for marriages these days? Fifty percent? I can't promise to succeed – I can only promise to try.'

'That will have to do. I'm promoting you to full colonel.'

'At this rate I'll be a general by the end of term.'

'A full general? But then you'd outrank me!'

'What rank are you?'

'Can't you guess?'

How could I have missed it?

'You are the very model of a modern major general.'

❧

Eighteen

'Come in, that's right!' exclaimed the mistress, gaily, pulling a chair to the fire.

You'd hear of odd things, if I lived alone with that mawkish, waxen face; the most ordinary would be painting on its white the colours of the rainbow.

And he stared hard at the object of discourse, as one might do at a strange repulsive animal, a centipede from the Indies, for instance, which curiosity leads one to examine in spite of the aversion it raises.

Returning home this evening, I saw the limo parked in front of the house and concluded that Gudrun had been successful. Half an hour later, Marie-Claire left and Heidi called down to invite me for a drink.

'Just one, Heidi – I have an early class.'

I was also reluctant to invite trouble by spending time with Gudrun.

'Class? It's the last week of term – no one teaches during the last week. Anyway, this is your head of department speaking, and you're still a wretched probationer – I order you!'

Heidi and Gudrun were giggling and smirking in the dining room. Both of them were dressed in blue, and even had blue lipstick.

'L'heure bleue,' Heidi enthused, handing me a martini glass with a blue drink in it. 'Vodka with Quebec blueberry liqueur. It's the latest craze.'

'Wonderful.' It sounded disgusting.

'A toast to Gudrun!'

'To Gudrun.'

'Gosh,' said Gudrun.

'And to tatouage!'

What now?

'Drink up and I'll explain.'

It was disgusting.

'Tatouage? Isn't that French for *tattooing*?'

They burst into giggles.

Drunks triumphant in the possession of a secret are exasperating. 'You won her back by having her name tattooed on your arm?'

'No – her soul!' cried Gudrun.

This they found even more hilarious.

I decided to give them a minute of silent query, finish my drink and go.

'Sorry, Will, it's just that ...' and they collapsed again. I rather thought I could smell weed in the air.

'It's just that you probably think Gudrun is a flake, a clumsy butterfly, but that flakiness and clumsiness mask a woman who is a semi-genius, so semi-cunning, so semi-devious that if they gave Nobel Prizes for con jobs, Gudrun would be this year's winner. To Gudrun Sigurdardóttir, Miss Volcano of 2002, and Nobel Semi-Laureate!'

They burst into giggles again. I looked at my watch and Heidi made an effort to be serious.

'What is the emblematic colour of Canada?'

'Red.'

'And Quebec?'

'Blue.'

'Correct. Now, what colour are my lips?'

'Blue. Blue lipstick? Or because of the drink?'

'It's blue lipstick. And you've seen my nipples – what colour are my they?'

'Red ... reddish brown.'

She smirked, and before I could protest she and Gudrun opened their fronts.

'Blue,' I said quietly. 'Blue in the shape of fleur-de-lys.'

'Blue, baby, patriotic Quebec blue,' said Heidi.

'I thought the Bourbon lilies were white?'

'Same difference – I'm not going to paint my boobs blue to show up the white fleur-de-lys. And ...' She began to lift her skirt.

'Enough, Heidi, I can guess.'

'Have you guessed Gudrun's semi-genius plan?'

'Well, it seems you have proved your loyalty to Quebec is above and beyond the call of duty, so she ...'

'No, no, no, nothing so simple. First, I'm not tattooed, of course, I am only demonstrating a possibility.'

'Okay. So next you'll ...'

'No, not just me, that's the genius of Gudrun's plan. She convinced Marie-Claire that as Ministre de la matrimonie et patrimonie sublime de la nation she should promote the idea to every Québécoise and Québécois.'

'Blue lipstick?'

'Well, sure, blue lipstick at first and for the timid, but you can't wear it under your clothes because it rubs off, so for those who are totally committed to the historic mission of the nation it's going to be blue tattooing on the three parts of the body which are most prominently red – lips, nipples, and lips! And the men – well, you can work it out for yourself, sweetie. Now, is that semi-genius or what?'

'It's semi-lunacy! No one will go for anything so crazy.'

'Wanna bet?'

'And by all accounts, Marie-Claire is an intelligent woman. Surely she didn't take it seriously?'

Heidi just shook her head in frustration. Gudrun, who had been silent, explained.

'This is Quebec, Will. Nothing, absolutely nothing is too kooky.'

'For example,' said Heidi, 'when the United Nations said Quebec's language laws contravened the Universal Declaration of Human Rights, the entire Quebec National Assembly resolved that *universal* applies everywhere in the universe except Quebec. And when ...'

'Yeah, yeah, Heidi, I've read Mordecai's essays, but the petty lunacy he describes is one thing – it's all a small band of nut cases on the street, empire builders inside the bureaucracy, some intellectuals. And no doubt the fonctionnaires and the tongue troopers are happy enough to have their jobs. But if Marie-Claire is going to make this tattooing nonsense work, she has to convince thousands of entirely sane women to ...'

'And men!'

'... women and men to mutilate their faces and their private parts in the name of nationalism. I don't believe it, and I can't believe Marie-Claire believes it either. She must have been letting the weed do her thinking.'

'Not only does she believe it, she's talking about the tongue, the eyelids, the toenails ...'

'Enough. I'll believe it when I see it.'

'Have another heure bleue.'

'What's the French for *disgusting*?'

'Dégoûtant. Yeah, it is, isn't it. But if Marie-Claire gets her way – and she always does – within two weeks every pure laine bar in the province will be promoting it during Happy Hour.'

'Surely you mean l'heure heureuse?'

'Naw, it's le Happy Hour. Or perhaps l'heure happy. Have a G&T instead. A beer?'

'Thanks, but I've got to be going.'

I stood up.

'Will,' Heidi said.

I turned. She was pulling up her hem. 'Are you sure you ...' in honeyed tones.

Giggles followed me as I bolted for the basement stairs.

Nineteen

I felt an irresistible yearning to be at the Heights.

This bed is the fairy cave under Penistone Crag.

I'm sure I should be myself were I once among the heather on those hills.

With the term over, we are all busy grading final exams and late papers, putting in book orders for next term, and attesting in quadruplicate (copies for the ministry, dean, department, teacher) that every writer we teach from Aeschylus to Zola was queer and/or of colour and/or a separatist. But the full pressure of classes is over. I've never lived in a big league ball town, so Margaret and I took in an Expos game. Last Saturday, we joined Harrison for *The Pirates of Penzance*, and Sunday we had dinner at a bring-your-own Thai restaurant.

'And did you get your add-on from Reykjavik to Edinburgh?' she asked over the green papaya salad.

'Yes, and I checked the web sites for the Festival and the Fringe – and I'm smack in the middle of them. Have you decided yet if you'll come too?'

'When you get home, call me and tell me your dates and flight numbers, then I'll call Icelandair first thing in the morning. Are you really sure I won't be in your way?'

Reassurances and kisses over the table.

'Is Harrison going on to Edinburgh with you?'

'No, he decided on Paris.'

'In August? Everyone in Paris will be away on holiday.'

'He said Paris is at its best when the Parisians are out of town.'

'He would say that.'

'And after I get my grades in I'll be working on the Smallweed paper. But what I'd really like to do is spend a week in Cape Breton in July during lobster season. I was there last summer before I came here, but it was August, so I missed the lobster.'

'Mmm ... fresh lobster,' she mused.

'Well, I'd offer to take you, but because of Harrison's lunatic jaunt, I can't even afford my own airfare to Nova Scotia, and we'd have to rent a car there, so I'm afraid it's Smallweed and daydreams.'

'Where would you stay?'

'My parents have a cottage in a place called Tobermory.'

'I'm afraid I've never heard of it.'

'It's on the west coast of Cape Breton – warm salt water beaches, mountains, fiddle music, dances, even a local single malt whisky – very Gaelic.'

'It sounds lovely.'

'It is.'

'Did you spend your summers there when you were growing up?'

'No, Mum and Dad used to rent a cottage on Mahone Bay near Halifax. They only bought this place when Dad retired a few years ago. It was an estate sale – owned by two little kids whose parents died and their guardians wanted to get rid of it.'

'Both parents died?'

'In separate car accidents as I recall, yes. Come to think it, I believe they lived in Montreal, or there was some Montreal connection.'

'I wonder if ... no.'

'You wonder what?'

'Nothing. A coincidence. Have you thought of driving to Nova Scotia instead of flying?'

'Rent here and drive the whole way?'

'No, what if you got a friend to drive you?'

'I doubt Harrison's heap could make it, and while Heidi would certainly cause a sensation on the beach, I'm not sure that I ...'

'Not Harrison, not Heidi.'

'Oops, I was a bit slow on that one, wasn't I? Your tone fooled me.'

'You're forgiven.'

'But that would be wonderful! My parents are going to England for July, so we'd have it all to ourselves. But I hadn't thought that you …'

'Don't think – just do.'

'Well, I …'

She touched a finger to my lips.

'Let me do the thinking for both of us – and the driving. And just to prove I'm competent outside the city, I'll take you on a magical mystery tour when this wretched weather warms up.'

'What's the mystery?'

'Can't you guess?'

When the warm weather arrived last week, Margaret telephoned to ask if I was free for a few days.

'Before me lie deserts of vast eternity.'

'You'll not need clothes for quite that long, but bring enough for three days, as well as some good walking shoes and sweaters and a jacket – the nights can be chilly.'

'We're staying overnight? Where?'

'More mystery.'

She picked me up just before nine. We crossed the Champlain Bridge to the south shore and drove east through flat farmland with the strange, isolated mountains I'd seen from Mount Royal. After half an hour, Margaret left the freeway and drove south through rolling hill country. We had lunch in a town called Sutton, then after more miles of hills and valleys, came to a grey stone and concrete monastery on a slope by a lake.

'The architect appears to have known the work of Charles Rennie Macintosh,' I remarked of the chapel.

'It could be. The Scottish-French connection, the Auld Alliance? I saw a whole Rennie Macintosh room in the Musée d'Orsay.'

In the monastery gift shop we stocked up on cheese and honey, then bought groceries in Knowlton.

'Just a few more miles.'

The name on the mailbox was 'Rowan.' The house, a hundred metres or so through the trees, had obviously been a farmhouse at some time in the past, but forest had taken over most of the fields and now the several clear acres were lawns and gardens.

'I expect Harrison has mentioned Eleanor and Magnus. They're on leave in London this year, both working on books. They left the keys with me so I could check the pipes and the heat every few weeks during the winter. In return, I get to stay in it whenever I want.'

'It's charming.'

'And to mow the lawn in the spring.'

'I believe that's what's meant by a pointed remark.'

'A broad hint. Tomorrow, perhaps. Let's get the groceries in, and while I put them in the fridge, you can bring in our bags. Then I want a quick shower.'

'Me too.'

After our showers, she led me out the door, through the flower garden, and past the fenced vegetable beds, forlorn with a winter's neglect.

'Beyond the strawberry patch there's an opening in the trees and a trail up along a brook. You'll see.'

As we got to the trees, I glanced back toward the house.

'Margaret, are you trying to lead me up the garden path?'

'What do you mean, *trying*?'

We followed the brook for a way, then took a branching path skirting the base of a cliff, then up, up, until we broke from the forest into a field crowning the hill.

'Come,' she beckoned, striding on upward through the young grass. In five minutes we were at the top.

'You bragged about the views of Cape Breton – how's this?'

Although higher hills rose to the southeast and southwest, between those ranges, and even more toward the north, we could see great distances. Margaret leaned against me.

'Away there, lost in the haze, is the St. Lawrence ... Knowlton and Brome Lake are over that hill ... over there a glimpse of Lake Memphremagog where Mordecai Richler lived during his last years ... Owl's Head is over that way ... Sutton and Jay Peak are beyond that ridge ...'

The air was rich with the scent of grasses and pines; it mingled with the scent of Margaret's hair. I bent to kiss her hair, her ear, the nape of her neck. She turned, lifted her lips to mine, and we sank slowly into the grass, embracing – cries, gasps, tears, the mystery revealed at last beneath the heavens.

In the evening we had steaks from the barbecue and sipped a Cabernet-Shiraz through the long twilight.

Outside, the night noises of the forest.

Inside, murmurs, caresses, sleep.

Margaret woke me with a coffee.

'I'm famished,' she said. 'I'm making us an enormous breakfast.'

'And we'll eat it on deck?'

'In the sun.'

We talked as vigorously as we ate. Later I mowed the lawn, then we drove into town and browsed through half a dozen craft and antique shops. I don't recall that we said anything particularly interesting through that long talky day or the next. Sometimes we were silent for minutes on end, but then we would find a subject and talk for an hour, all the usual chat of academics – books, movies, eccentric professors, interesting fellow students, cities we had visited. All the usual chat of new lovers – childhood scrapes, teenage angst, our families – kept us smiling, chuckling, laughing, sometimes thoughtful, serious, even passionate about the subject.

The last morning I managed to slip gently from the bed without waking her. The aroma of the coffee brought movement, moans, the sleepy embrace of a woman whose slim body and tousled hair suggested guileless youth. Her shy, affectionate, wordless merriment lasted through the first cup of coffee. Compared with the austere, efficient woman at the college, this Margaret was unexpected – I was, am besotted.

'Time to clean up and get back to town.'

'I've enjoyed every minute of it.'

I reached across to take her hand.

'So did I, Will, so did I.'

'I'll ask again – do you suppose this is how a perfect marriage would be?'

She took a sip, looked away.

'Perhaps ... yes.'

'Which implies I should either make a joke of it with *while it lasts* or *perfection is denied humankind* or I should propose to you.'

'Let's make a joke of it.'

'Why am I not surprised?'

'For a while yet.'

'Let's say goodbye here,' she said when she dropped me out front. 'I want to get away without being seen by Miss Green Bay Packers or Miss Geological Catastrophe.'

In her embrace she softened, hiding her face in my neck, and murmuring endearments.

'Soon again?' I asked through the car window.

'Soon again.'

I waved till her car was around the corner.

'Soon again,' I repeated, with a silly grin on my face. 'Soon again.'

Twenty

She came forward eagerly to greet me; and held out one hand.

I have discovered I have very little idea what to do with a woman besides have dinner, talk, or see a movie. Watching more than two or three hours of television a week has always struck me as evidence of a debased character. One museum visit a month is about all I can take, and I can't afford concerts – rock, classical or jazz – although Margaret says there'll be a jazz festival soon with all sorts of free concerts and we might give them a try. In the meantime, she registered us both in the Tour de l'isle, the bicycle rally.

'Fifty k by bike on Montreal streets? It would be suicide!'

'No, they close the streets to traffic. And we'll have 50,000 allies.'

'I don't have a bike. I suppose I could buy one?'

'Heidi will lend you her old one – she needs a new one, without the crossbar. Now, the start is east of the mountain. We could bike it, but I suggest we take our bikes on the Metro ...'

So it was that we exited from the Fabre station about nine-thirty and cycled down Papineau looking for the start. The morning was cool, mostly cloudy, and a bit windy, but it was comfortable enough, and we soon joined the stream of cyclists. The first twenty minutes or so were through streets of crowded houses and small shops.

'Trivia quiz,' said Margaret. 'What word would Graham Greene have used for this neighbourhood?'

'*Seedy*. Try something difficult?'

'Give me time.'

Light rain began as we entered the Botanical Gardens.

'Charming,' said Margaret as we approached the rest area. 'Somebody has narrowed the route from eight wide to three wide?'

Hundreds of cyclists had dismounted and were creeping toward a narrow opening with marshals along the funnel to be sure no one took a shortcut across the grass.

« 145 »

'Obviously the Quebec highways department is on the job,' she added.

When we mounted again, we found ourselves approaching the Olympic Stadium.

'Next question: what cartoonist first pictured the Big O as a toilet?'

'I don't know. I suppose it must be the guy in the *Gazette*.'

'Aislin. Right.'

As the rain was obviously going to continue, we stopped and put on our waterproof tops.

'At least the route hasn't had any serious hills yet.'

'No, and from the map, I think there are only two, and neither is serious.'

On St Catherine East now, we rode easily in the stream of bikes.

'Third question: in Montreal, what can't you throw a rock without hitting?'

'A tavern?'

'No. Second guess.'

'A women's shoe store?'

'Very funny. Last chance.'

'A sarcastic woman?'

'Beast. The answer is a church.'

'Big deal – try it in Edinburgh.'

'But in Edinburgh all the churches have been converted to discos or condos?'

'Hey, Margaret, rain or not, I'm really enjoying this.'

We chatted about the shops, bars and churches. And about the variety of bikes – kiddie trailers, supine pedallers, tandems and quads, a unicyclist in a clown suit.

'Folk really get into this, don't they?'

'I think there are prizes for costumes. I wonder if Astérix and Obélix will score.'

'How about the guy with the Jean Chrétien mask?'

'Not a chance.'

Instead of passing through central downtown, the route turned left through Old Montreal to the port area, under the Lachine Canal, then through another area of modest houses and warehouses converted to condominiums. As the last of the drizzle died away, we climbed a short hill to a park with the second rest area. Margaret coasted to a stop.

'The clouds are going – let's stop and take off the rain gear.'

Although the wind was still chilly we found a sheltered place in the sun, and sat to eat some clementines.

'Lovely view,' I said. 'Is that factory for paint or cement?'

Then Margaret grabbed my arm.

'Omygod, it can't be ... it must be ... it is!'

I followed her point – there on a blue tandem rode Marie-Claire and Heidi.

From a pole mounted at the back streamed a banner: *La vie en bleue!*

With great blue-lipsticked grins on their faces they pulled to a stop and dismounted. Marie-Claire wore blue leather pants with blue knee-length boots, Heidi a blue miniskirt with blue pantyhose and blue boots. Both sported blue sunglasses and blue berets on their blue hair.

I have not mentioned their tops.

They were not wearing tops.

They were bare from hip to hair.

And over their nipples they had lipsticked blue fleurs-de-lys.

Behind them came Gudrun and fifty or more similarly attired acolytes flourishing *La vie en bleue* banners. Spotting us, Gudrun swerved to join us, and half a dozen acolytes behind her went to the ground in a tangle of limbs, bikes, banners and nipples. Heidi came tottering over with arms spread.

'Darlings!' she cried.

'Gee, hi!' from Gudrun.

'Good morning, Heidi ... Gudrun,' said Margaret.

'Isn't it a bit chilly for ... all this?' I asked.

'Chilly!' said Heidi. 'Mon pays ce n'est pas un pays, c'est l'hiver! I'm big enough that I can take it, but look at Gudrun, or poor Marie-Claire, such a slip of a thing, her nips are standing out like spikes. Of course, my rings are like icicles, you can't imagine!'

'I can imagine,' said Margaret.

'But it's all in a good cause – great banners, eh? Some arty types at the ministry ran them up for Marie-Claire.'

'Very clever.'

'Why don't you join us, Margaret? Whip your top off – we have tons of lipstick. Gudrun, can you help Marie-Claire?'

Gudrun grabbed a bag from her bike and began pressing lipsticks on the unadorned women gathered about Marie-Claire.

'Another time, perhaps.'

'Oh, Megs, you're such a drip – you ought to live a little – where's your sense of adventure? Anyway, sorry darlings, have to run!'

Gudrun and the acolytes were busily converting others to the great cause – all around the rest area women were pulling off their tops and applying the fleur-de-lys to one another.

'I expect you want to stay and enjoy the show,' said Margaret.

Marie-Claire was fiddling with a bullhorn.

'No thanks – I already know women have nipples.'

Margaret scrutinized my face.

Marie-Claire found the right switch; she made a remark, shook her meagre breasts, and provoked general laughter among the women and the few men gathered about her. Most of the men in the area were either ogling breasts, studying the sky, or kicking tires.

'A speech from Marie-Claire? Will, let's get out of here.'

The *Gazette* had but a brief mention of 'an initiative by Marie-Claire Piché, Minister of the Immortal Soul and the Sacred Blood of the People', and discreetly limited itself to a mention of 'fleur-de-lys body art'. But Heidi summoned me upstairs for a coffee and a perusal of a French tabloid which featured a front page colour photo of Mlle La Ministre herself with bullhorn and blue nipples. Behind and slightly out of focus, Heidi was visible.

'Well, Heidi, you're certainly better endowed than Marie-Claire.'

'It's not how big they are, babe, but what you do with them. Marie-Claire's are tasty little morsels, sort of like hors d'oeuvres. Anyway, let me read you what the story says … You'll have to excuse the translation, I have to adapt it to get the alliteration – "Similar shows are planned for the fête nationale. Ripe ones from Rouyn to Rimouski … tiny ones from Tadoussac to Témiscaming … slinky ones from Saglouc to Sherbrooke … plans for decorations that will belittle Christmas … Rumours abound about the Big O" …'

'The Big O?'

'Not the big orgasm – the Olympic Stadium. When we cycled past it yesterday, I told Marie-Claire it looked like a gigantic breast in a ribbed bra cup, sort like a Valkyrie's, and she thought it was a great idea. Paint a giant fleur-de-lys on the plastic roof and light it from inside – imagine that at night – a billion dollar boob with seating for fifty thousand! And some sort of lace motif sprayed on the shell – Montreal has lots of lingerie manufacturers who would be glad to pay the cost.'

'They would? I thought profit margins were tight in the garment industry.'

'Get serious, babe, this is Quebec. If the government suggests the shmatte trade pony up a few shekels for support – support ha-ha, – it's a matter of "I need three volunteers – you, you, and you." If they refuse, the company's books and the owners' income tax returns are audited by Monsieur Ebenezer de la Scrooge and the arrears collected by Monsieur Rambo, and I don't mean the poet. Anyway, the government will be providing most of the money.'

'I'm glad to hear my tax dollars are going to a worthy cause.'

'Causes, babe, causes. Montreal is a city of festivals and Marie-Claire is going to take *La vie en bleue* to all of them – fireworks, jazz, comedy, film, and those are just the biggies. But the best one, so far as Marie-Claire and I are concerned, is Divers/Cité in July.'

'Divers-itay?'

She spelled it out. 'It's Gay Pride Week. You absolutely must catch the parade, babe, the costumes are almost as good as the ones in the Caribbean parade, it's in July, too. Poor Marie-Claire, she has to attend all of them, of course, and I've only mentioned the Montreal ones – the whole province goes festival crazy during the summer – the little sweetie is just run ragged, she's an Amazon for culture.'

'I'm beginning to understand.'

'And how she's going to fit in the Iceland trip is beyond me.'

'Marie-Claire is coming too?'

'Gudrun's been on to her – an ancient prophecy of some sort – well, you know Gudrun – she's always up to something.'

A crash on the stairs.

« 149 »

'Shit, what's she broken this time?'

'It wasn't my fault, really!' she called as her footsteps descended, 'The statue just leaped off the shelf.'

Heidi leaned toward me.

'Did she really burn down that house in Aarhus?' she whispered.

'It's not broken!' Gudrun called from the hall.

'I believe it was judged to be an act of God.'

'Another reason we have to get rid of Him. That house would still be standing if we worshipped the Goddess.'

'You mean I'd get to blame Her for everything?'

'Pig.'

'Are you two ready for a revelation?' Gudrun called from the hall. 'I want you to be the first to see.'

'What in hell's name are you blathering about, you silly woman?'

'Not silly, new – I'm a new woman. Or perhaps I should say, I'm a new girl.'

Heidi looked at me and shrugged.

'You'll no longer be a walking disaster? You're going to stop breaking things? I won't have to double my fire insurance?'

'Don't be so negative, Heidi. Anyway, this is more about a body and soul rebirth. Don't you want to see?'

'Can we avoid it?'

'Okay, well you know that I'm a völva, and in preparation for assuming the role seriously, I've had to purify myself.'

Heidi whispered, 'For your sake, Will, I hope this has nothing to do with tampons.'

'Okay, ready or not, here I come!'

Gudrun bounded into the room and jumped to a stop:

'Ta-dah! Behold, Gudrun reborn!'

Not only was she naked, she was entirely hairless, and with three appropriately placed Icelandic flags in lipstick.

'Tinks! What have you done to Tinker Bell?'

In her arms Gudrun carried Tinker Bell – also hairless, and with a blue fleur-de-lys on her back and sides.

Twenty-One

I pondered, and worried myself to discover what it could be; and, most strangely, the whole last seven years of my life grew a blank!

Her appearance is changed greatly, her character much more so; and the person who is compelled, of necessity, to be her companion, will only sustain his affection hereafter by the remembrance of what she once was.

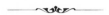

After an afternoon walk on the beach, in the last light of the sun, we ate lobster on the deck overlooking the cove. Margaret lifted her wine glass to an osprey making a last dive:

'Di Provenza il mar, il suol. All right, I admit it, Cape Breton is more beautiful than the Eastern Townships.'

She gazed at me.

'Will, I think I love you.'

'I think I love you, Margaret.'

She stood up.

'Come along, then.'

Now she lies asleep, at peace. I slipped from the bed and brought the laptop out onto the deck. The full moon, high in the west, silvers the cove and the distant fields and hills. Round the corner of the cottage, I picked out the Big Dipper, and so to the North Star and the W of Cassiopeia. The Milky Way streams down to the horizon before me. And that is the limit of my knowledge. What are these three bright stars directly overhead? The previous owners left a star guide, along with a copy of *The Birds of Nova Scotia*. Perhaps I'll look at it tomorrow.

Blinking fireflies in the meadow before me.

Among the stars, blinking lights passing from west to east – an airliner out of Boston or New York, perhaps, heading for Europe.

As the plane's lights grow smaller to the east, the burr of its engines following far behind the lights.

From beyond the hill, the drone of a car on the main road, someone late home from a dance perhaps.

But the engine noises are unnatural additions to the night sounds. The lap of waves on the shore. Frogs croaking from a pond … other animals or insects, unknown to me. In the occasional breeze, the clicking of poplar leaves, the gentle whoosh of spruce boughs.

The creak of bedsprings.

She is probably turning in the bed.

A door closing.

Flushing toilet.

The woman I love is awake.

That was three days ago. The stars were fading in the first hints of dawn before we again found sleep.

On her way out to the deck, Margaret picked up the bottle of whisky, a carafe of water, and two glasses. She set a glass on my side of the little table, then poured one for herself.

'I love you,' I said.

After a long minute, she replied softly, 'I love you.'

She took a sip of Scotch.

A silent presence glided from the trees to the left, made a low pass over the meadow, disappeared in the trees to the right.

'What was that?' she asked.

'An owl I think.'

'Does Athene lend her wisdom to this night?'

She turned toward me. Her voice came from a pale smudge in the shadows.

'Will, there's something I want to tell you before this goes any further.'

'There's nothing you have to tell me, Margaret.'

'I know you mean that, and perhaps I shouldn't, but I think I must. I'm nervous because it's going to shock you.'

'Margaret, I don't care about it, whatever it is – I sense it's gone. Keep your secret. I love you here and now.'

'So you knew there was a secret?'

'Harrison must have told you – I've wondered sometimes about a something, a presence just beyond my vision. A man, a lover I supposed. I rather guessed a rich and powerful married man. Something like that. It doesn't interest me, his identity doesn't interest me.'

'It's not a him. It's more than one.'

'I've not been exactly chaste myself.'

'In fact it has been quite a few.'

'Gudrun strikes me as widely ... adventurous. And Harrison. And Heidi.'

'Will, have you wondered about one of Harrison's nicknames for me – the Black Orchid?'

'I've heard him use it.'

'He means I'm rare and expensive. For the past eight years I've been working as an escort.'

I had a brief picture of Margaret in a uniform helping pensioners off a tour bus. But she obviously meant something else.

'You mean you go out with visiting businessmen to ... that sort of thing?'

'That sort of thing.'

'Including ...?'

'Including sex, yes. Will, I'm a prostitute.'

'You're ...'

'Perhaps I may say I *was* a prostitute. I retired at the end of January. Admit it, you're shocked.'

I surprised myself – I arose and went to her, embraced her, kissed her, gazed into the shadows of her eyes.

'No,' I said at last. 'I admit I am surprised. But not shocked.'

'Not ...'

'I love you more, more than before.'

Her voice floated in the darkness, calm now, matter-of-fact, for it was no longer her secret, but ours.

'After I left Harrison, I went to Toronto for my master's. I expected a fellowship, but it didn't come through. Budget adjustments, they told me. I was alone, and broke, and a bit depressed. Of course, I applied for a student loan, but the first instalment was months away. Then one day I ran into a girl I'd known at McGill. She was doing sociology. Let's say her name was Monika. I told her my situation and we talked about the possibilities – library jobs, waitressing, that sort of thing. She said she was doing all right, something in the hospitality trade, hotels, but she wasn't specific, and changed the subject. A few evenings later we went for drinks, and she dropped a few hints. I guessed at once. She admitted she had been an escort for most of the past winter. I was briefly shocked, but I found I was curious. Don't believe everything the feminists tell you – at one time or another most girls fantasize about being a prostitute, if only for a night.

'I was surprised when she explained that prostitution, taking money for sex, is legal in Canada. Lots of aspects of it are illegal – soliciting, keeping a common bawdy house, living off the avails, underage girls – but not the exchange itself. That was a relief.

'Monika told me how it worked. She was with an agency. They took the calls, they'd call her, she'd go to the hotel, meet the client, and an hour later leave with $200.

'At those prices, and since it's in hotels, the clients are from out of town. Some are executives, but most have their own businesses. Monika said they're under a lot of pressure, they feel a little lonely, a little macho, and just want an hour or two with an attractive, compliant young woman and they can afford to pay for it. They're reasonably well behaved; if the girl can carry on an intelligent conversation and is presentable – if she doesn't actually look like a prostitute – they may invite her for the evening – a drink, a meal in a nearby restaurant, then an hour or two upstairs. And every hour at the same price.

'She said she'd go with me the first time, and if I couldn't go through with it I could leave and she would carry on. She made it seem very civilized. Of course, there was the question of being paid to have sex with a stranger, but it seemed … possible, do-able.

'So the next day Monika introduced me at the agency, and that evening I saw my first client. Within two weeks I was seeing four or five clients a week.

'I found I was good at it. The challenge wasn't the sex – the physical was an accepted fact – it was the encounter that interested me, intrigued me. I found I wanted to seduce the mind – I had to be a actress, a psychologist, a diplomat, a good listener, a companion, even a friend. I didn't want to make them fall in love with Margaret –

they weren't meeting Margaret – but I did want them to fall in love, however briefly, with Julia – yes, that's my evening name.

'And I was successful beyond my wildest dreams. Within a few months I had more requests than I could handle – I was turning them down. The agency didn't much like that, because they were one of the biggest in town, they spent a lot on advertising, and they wanted to make the most of the opportunities. So Monika and Julia moved to a smaller, more easygoing agency that specialized in discreet, educated girls, many of them students. They understood that during term we couldn't always be free. So I had solved my financial problems.'

For some minutes we were silent, while around us the night creatures croaked and chirped, and the moon and the stars moved imperceptibly across the sky.

'You're not ... repelled?'

Margaret's words hung in the dark.

'Well ... as I said, I guessed you had a secret, and it probably involved a lover. One knows some women are ... escorts, but just as you were surprised by your friend Monika, I was surprised by Julia. But I fell in love with Margaret, not Julia. Margaret is here, and Julia is somewhere else. Now that I know Margaret's secret, I find I still love her. I'm not thinking, really, I'm just trying to feel what I feel.'

This time she arose and came to me and sat in my lap and snuggled against me.

Her tears fell hot on my cheek.

More tears and many words passed in the moonlight, the starlight of that night, and many kisses touched, brushed, crushed our lips over the next days while we walked the beaches as the wind filled the skies with the boom of surf, as the moon rose over the distant hills, lit up the trees, the fields, the waters of the cove, and glimmered in glasses of white wine.

'I can see why you were nervous,' I said over coffee one evening, 'but the problem must have been there from the beginning – if you meet a man you want to marry, do you keep it quiet, or do you risk telling him?'

'Yes. At the beginning I was wounded from my break-up with Harrison; I was down on marriage, engagements, anything long term. But I didn't hate men, and I soon enough saw that in time I would likely meet someone I cared for, wanted to care for. That's when I began to wonder seriously about telling. When I was feeling good, I'd say to myself, Damn it, if he really loves me, he'll have to take it, and if he can't, he's not worth it. But when the schoolwork was getting to me, on grey winter days, I'd vow never to admit it. Why cause trouble? I'd ask myself, Why risk everything, if it's all over? But I was never certain what I would do. That was fine as long as it was in the future.'

'Maybe my intuition is wrong, but I sense you must have told Harrison.'

'He knows, but I didn't tell him, and he didn't guess – or he claims he didn't.'

'Then …'

'Gudrun told him, of course. Shortly after she started at the college, he had us both to dinner. I think he thought we might be friends – his intuition is usually good on such matters, but she started blathering about "I am a seeress, heir to ancient Icelandic wisdom." "Prove it," he said, "Tell us Meg's most cherished secret." She answered immediately, "Oh, you mean that she's a prostitute?" I don't know whether she was just making an insulting guess, or whether she had seen me in some hotel lobby meeting a client. She certainly didn't learn it from reading runes.'

'How did Harrison react?'

'Superbly: "Oh, everyone knows Megs has a sideline in the horizontal profession – I meant the *real* secret – that she writes poetry. Now tell me mine." So she said he was impotent, and we all had a laugh about that and the conversation drifted to other things.'

'Do you think he believed her?'

'I asked him a few days later. "Prostitution is not the exchange of sex for money, Megs, it's a state of mind. You couldn't be a prostitute, not even if you were peddling it wholesale at the corner of St Cat's and the Main." And resolutely refused to discuss it further.'

'When did you decide to retire – to make the past past?'

'I decided for certain during Christmas dinner – it was when you were talking about the striptease Harrison's daughters did and the wet T-shirt contest. I thought, If this man can deal with this, he can deal with my escort work – he is worthy of trust. Maybe I'll discover he's not the man for me, but now I know it is possible. And at once I felt comfortable and peaceful, and I liked that.'

'So why ... uhh ...'

'Why the delay? Because I wanted to have every single test to be sure everything was okay. I got the final test result just before we spent those days in the Townships. Of course, I'd been thinking about retiring for a few years, and for the last year or so I'd only been seeing old regulars. They were comfortable to be with ... clients, of course, but old friends, too ... and they're very generous. You may recall that I wasn't able to see you Thanksgiving weekend?'

'Yes.'

'I was in New Orleans. And I was hoping you weren't watching the ball drop in Times Square on New Year's Eve.'

'A nice little treat.'

'Plus *Don Carlo*, *Die Frau Ohne Schatten* and *La Bohème* at the Met. I was hoping for *La Traviata* – a sort of goodbye to the business – but we missed it by a couple of days.'

'Excuse me for being crass, but at $200 an hour? For a whole weekend? That must have been ...'

'I gave a flat rate – $5000. US.'

'My God, Margaret – these guys must be really rich.'

'That one is an investment banker ...'

I don't think of myself as particularly subtle or tactful, so it's a miracle I have managed to sense that I should not joke about, should not even mention our time together in terms of money – it is worth everything, it is worth nothing, it is beyond price. At least I have noticed that Margaret does not do it either.

'Just after Christmas I sent e-mails to my few remaining clients telling them I was retiring. Most of them accepted it – I'd been talking about it for a while – but several of them begged me to see them one last time, so I extended the deadline to the end of January. And then, apart from the tests, it really was over.'

I remembered the evening last fall when we met for a late drink and Margaret arrived wearing make-up, a cocktail dress, dressy boots – more dressed up even than she was at Christmas. Now I realized she had come from a client. 'Am I offended?' I asked myself. I found I wasn't. Amazingly, I was rather flattered that she would take the chance that her dress might arouse my suspicions, yet instead of calling me at the bar to cancel she came anyway. I haven't mentioned this either.

Yesterday afternoon we went for a walk along the ocean-side cliffs, and stopped under some trees on a promontory. As we lay side by side, I realized something, and wondered if I should keep it to myself. A sudden conviction prompted me to speak.

'Margaret, I don't know what this means, but I've known of your evening work for over two days, yet I find my imagination is not interested in picturing you with your clients.'

She shaded her eyes and looked at me quizzically.

'I mean, it's as if I'm running movies in my head. I have imagined you being charming and witty in expensive restaurants that I'll never be able to take you to, I've imagined you flying business class, or sipping a long drink on a terrace in the French Quarter in New Orleans, or striding coolly across a hotel lobby toward the elevators. I have even imagined you entering the room and calling the 'I'm inside' confirmation to the agency, but it ends there. I wonder why?'

'That's more than I could expect. Are you just saying it to reassure me?'

'No, actually, I'm trying to figure it out for myself.'

I raised myself on my elbows and gazed toward the horizon, lost in the bluish heat haze of late afternoon.

'I think … maybe it's that I've never thought of sex as I suppose an escort must, as an end in itself, as something isolated from the rest of … of life, of love. Do you remember I once said that I've never been much interested in making love with a woman I wouldn't consider marrying?'

'Yes. It was very sweet of you. And perhaps ever so slightly naive.'

'Thanks for the trenchant exegesis, Dr Taylor, I'll do the same for you sometime. No, I mean that for me lovemaking is something that comes after love flowers, after a day, an hour of affection, it's the result of love, not a thing in itself. I've never quite understood guys who see a pretty girl in a bar and say, "Whoa, catch that babe – I'd love to get into her panties!" Obviously, I could see that she was attractive, but I've always wondered, What books does she like, what paintings, what music? What would we talk about over the breakfast table?'

'Crude but apt.'

'So it seems that, for my imagination at least, what went on in those hotel rooms was … I don't know … irrelevant, I guess.'

Margaret put her finger to my lips.

'Let's see if what goes on beneath the fir trees on a bluff above a sunlit ocean is irrelevant.'

'Again?'

Twenty-Two

Find a way, then! Not through that Kirkyard.

But though Isabella Linton may be silly, she is scarcely mad.

On the drive back to Montreal, we sometimes talked about what we had come to call her nights out with Julia. We talked not of the work itself, but of the accidentals – clothes, make-up, the best hotels, her favourite restaurants, some of her trips. She was chattering – Margaret chattering! – about a ski jaunt to Whistler when I interrupted,

'From the way you talk, I think you enjoyed the work.'

'I told you, it was a challenge, and if I hadn't enjoyed that, I would have quit after a few weeks. I was very good at it. Frankly, I feel more like a whore teaching great literature to kids who don't want to read it than I ever felt as an escort.'

'Marry me.'

'Yes.'

I shall be moving in with Margaret after we get back from Iceland and Gudrun will return to this flat. Margaret has spoken of getting married on New Year's Day. To celebrate, Heidi took me for a smoked meat sandwich at Schwartz's.

'This is very generous of you,' I said to her when the waiter set the plates before us.

'Haven't you ever had a smoked meat sandwich before? Real Montreal smoked meat?'

'Sure. You can get Montreal smoked meat in most any supermarket in Canada.'

She sighed.

'Smoked meat has the mysterious quality that if it leaves the island of Montreal it ceases to be smoked meat. I'm not even convinced it can travel safely east of St Denis or west of the Decarie Expressway. People say it can be found in Beaconsfield or DDO or some such West Island bidonville, but I have my doubts. Smoked meat from Schwartz's or the Snowdon Deli is a crucial element in the heart of Montreal – you can't be a real Montrealer until you have eaten it at least once a month for ten years.'

One taste convinced me – smoked meat that leaves the island ceases to be smoked meat.

'But I thought the heart of Montreal is supposed to be French, not eastern European Jewish?'

'Le smoked meat is French, it's Jewish, it's Romanian – who cares? Smoked meat is Montreal. Anyway, congratulations, you're finally on your way to becoming a Montrealer.'

'Thank you.'

'Besides, I'm hoping marriage will soften the Black Death. As it is, she's either dripping silent poison on people, or she's wandering around in distracted melancholy like someone out of the Brontës. Just make sure you keep her well bonked.'

'Don't be crude.'

'And don't you be prissy. Anyway, the sooner Gudrun can move back into her old place and out of mine, the better – she's already trashed three of my hedgehogs and the shower door, and one of the dining room chairs is out for repair. Not to mention shaving my little Tinks, and wounding poor Marie-Claire while she was shaving her the other day. And it wasn't her armpits, poopsie.'

'Spare me the details. But how is Marie-Claire otherwise?'

'I have to admit I'm really worried about her. Since the failure of the Blue Tattoo campaign, the poor dear has been frantic to find something to promote the great cause. Gudrun has convinced her the answer is in Iceland, but I don't know. If nothing else, we're going to be married there.'

'Congratulations. I guess I'll have to start thinking about a wedding gift.'

'You could replenish my collection of thousand-year eggs,' and rather ghoulishly chomped off a length of dill pickle.

'Or I could not. Sometimes I wonder how complete your transition to the feminine has been?'

'You can take the girl out of the locker room, but you can't take the locker room out of the girl.'

'I think I'll stick with towels or pillow slips for the wedding gift. You'll have to give me a list.'

'How about I skip a gift for you and Margaret, and you skip ours? Anyway, that's the least of my problems. See, we haven't yet decided to marry as man and wife, man and man, or wife and wife.'

'I thought Gudrun talked Marie-Claire out of getting the operation?'

'Operations plural, sweetie. She did, but Marie-Claire isn't sure now. You see, just a few weeks ago, Quebec became the second province – after Nova Scotia, quelle mortification! – to recognize gay and lesbian civil unions. But of course a civil union is not a marriage.'

'Civil unions? Isn't that just a marriage in city hall?'

'No, that's a civil marriage. A civil union is about pensions and survivor's rights and stuff like that. But just the other day, an Ontario court ruled that gay marriages must be made legal, but they've given Ottawa two years to change the law, so I gather it will apply across Canada, but that's another delay. The Netherlands recognizes gay marriages, but it's the only EU country that does. Perhaps the marriage wouldn't be valid in Canada, but maybe it will if others follow – some EU court ruled last week that transsexuals can marry people of their former sex, but Marie-Claire isn't my former sex, not unless she has the operation, but perhaps *I* would then be considered *her* former sex, or perhaps *my* former sex would apply, but if it did, so would Marie-Claire's, in which case *I* would be the husband even though *I'm* a woman, and *she* would be the wife, even though *she* would be a man, and then ... But it's all too complicated for *me – I'm* just your typical flighty feminoid with no sense of the practical world.'

'Well, it is complicated.'

'But we have definitely decided to go for at least the civil union – I mean, sweetie, those Assemblée Nationale porkers *really* have their snouts in the trough. If Marie-Claire retired *today*, her pension would be twice my salary! Hell, when we have a civil union, even I will be eligible for a spousal pension that's bigger than my salary, never mind my pension. But what is government but a trough for the care and feeding of the elected members and their hangers-on?'

Heidi contemplated the last bits of rye bread with the slices of spicy meat between them.

'Great, eh?'

'Superb.'

She popped it into her mouth.

'Eat it, savour it, as it is set before you. That's how to take Quebec.'

'I'm learning.'

'Yeah, you seem to be pretty broad-minded, but you're young – for your generation, it's a new world.'

She lowered her voice.

'I just wish Marie-Claire would loosen up. She's fine on gender issues, but I have to admit she's a tiny bit intolerant on language. But I'm working on her, convincing her that all this feudal crap about the two solitudes is dead. Two solitudes, three, four – who cares? Who cares about French-English any more? We're all one. Who cares about male-female any more? We're all one. Who cares about your money–my money? It's all one. Did you know Quebec has more employees in the Ministry of Education than any other jurisdiction in the civilized world? On a per capita basis. It's about the same in every other ministry. Someday, everyone in Quebec will be an employee of the Quebec government.'

The burly man just behind her had put down his sandwich and was listening with growing amazement.

'That's what's wrong with all the dinosaurs, everyone from wee Bernie Landry to big Brent Tyler, from the SSJB to the Eeks, they all think in exclusive units – 'I am an Anglo, she is French' – but why can't you be both? 'I am a man,' you think, 'therefore I must love and marry a woman.' But why not love another man? Why Margaret and not Harrison, for example?'

'Too old for me.'

'Or why not *become* a woman? And if she wants, why shouldn't Margaret become a man? Frankly, with her personality, I think she'd do far better as a man. Anyway sweetie, it's no accident that Quebec is a world leader in transsexual operations. It's sooo Quebec!'

The burly man said, 'Lady, you're bananas.'

Heidi picked up the man's sandwich and pasted it on his face.

'And if I had a banana I'd show you what to do with it, asshole.'

The man pulled back his arm to swing at her, but Heidi was quicker, landing a left on the man's nose. He fell back with blood streaming down.

'I may be a lady,' said Heidi as we rose to go, 'but I also played for the good old Fuddpuckers. You should have seen the Nimblenuts after we were finished with them in the '63 Brawling Bowl. Not a pretty sight.'

'I thought you were a cheerleader.'

'Naughty boy – no, I was a centre linebacker.'

Heidi elbowed me in the ribs.

'And you should have seen *their* cheerleaders after we were finished with them. We called that the Balling Bowl.'

'I don't think I want to hear about it.'

'You don't – they were not a pretty sight either. There were great racks on some of them, but broads all look the same with a helmet on!'

When I dropped by to give Harrison his Icelandair tickets, he invited me through for a drink in the dappled shade of his back yard.

'A congratulatory drink, in fact, on your promotion to brigadier for making it through a year in our lunatic asylum.'

'The school isn't that bad.'

'I meant Quebec. And for your successful proposal to Dr Megs:

> 'Let the air with joy be laden,
> Rend with songs the air above,
> For the union of a maiden
> With the man who owns her love.'

'She has indeed been kind enough to agree to honour me with her hand.'

'I'm sure other bodily parts come with it.'

'You're as crude as Heidi.'

'And Megs says you don't seem bothered by her other career.'

I didn't want to discuss it.

'No, I seem not to be. But you don't seem bothered by it either.'

'Why should I be? It has nothing to do with me.'

'Or with me. But she loves you, Harrison, more than she loves me, I think.'

He closed his eyes and waved his hand vaguely.

'Pass the vinho verde, Brigadier Ass.'

'You've been on to me all winter to marry her – why don't you marry her?'

'Three strikes and you're out – I've got four and a half strikes against me.'

'And you love her – I'm certain of it.'

'I do indeed. Very dear to me, the Black Orchid is, but I'll not make her the Black Widow.'

'Stop playing with words.'

'I'm saying I'm too old – or doesn't your knowledge of literary theory run to allusion. Or is that hyperbole? Or synecdoche?'

'You're fifteen years older than Margaret – that's not a hopeless difference.'

'It's closer to twenty, and you're trying to wriggle out of your engagement, you snake.'

'No, I'm trying to understand why Margaret is willing to marry me instead of you.'

'I have nothing you haven't got, Brigadier, except you'll have twenty more years in this vale of tears.'

I wanted to mention charm, wit, experience, sex appeal, but settled for, 'I think you'd be more likely to … to be able to keep her happy … contented.'

'You mean well bonked.'

'No, I don't.'

'Okay, you mean wit and all that, but you also mean bonking, but … well, perhaps some other time.'

What now?

'But what about Iceland? By Thor, I wonder if the sight of a spouting volcano … no … Are you prepared? How's your Icelandic coming? Talarðu íslensku?'

'Já, en bara pínulítið, takk fyrir.'

'Excellent. And what is the one essential phrase?'

'Eitt bjor, gerðu svo vel.'

'Make it tveir bjor and we're in business. Now, what's this non-sense about flying via Boston?'

Twenty-Three

He was a plain, rough man.

It *was* rather a rough mess, I own.

He's not a rough diamond – a pearl-containing oyster of a rustic; he's a fierce, pitiless, wolfish man.

We were well into our third round in the bar nearest the Icelandair departure gate at Logan when Margaret said, 'Guys, the last flight they could have taken from Montreal arrived over an hour ago. If the three wyrd sisters are coming with us, they'd better get here soon.'

'In a perfect world,' said Harrison, 'they'd be half way to Rwanda.'

'Guðrún said they'd meet us here two hours before departure.'

(I might as well spell it *Guðrún* since I'm writing this in Iceland.)

'Iraq perhaps. Afghanistan still has possibilities.'

'For God's sake, Harrison, what are you babbling about?'

'As long as it's a pestilential shithole with poisonous snakes, bad water, crotch rot and a civil war.'

'Perhaps they're going via Newark,' I said.

'Yes, Newark would do.'

'I read a biography of MacArthur once,' said Margaret, 'and New Guinea sounded pretty nasty.'

'Are they having a civil war just now?'

'Not that I recall. But the place is nasty enough without a war – everything rots.'

'Is it Islamic?'

'That's ethnic profiling.'

'Not guilty, m'lud – I just want them rotting without the solace of cold beer. And it's the brigadier's round, I believe.'

* * *

'Enjoy the sunshine while you've got it,' said Harrison as we made our way along the arrivals concourse, 'because the odds are seven to four that we get rain tomorrow.'

Margaret swung her purse at him.

'Now he tells me.'

Iceland has the civilized practice of allowing duty-free purchases on the way into the country, so we did some banking and looked about the shops.

'How much is this straight malt in Canadian?' Harrison asked.

Margaret thought a moment. 'Just under $58.'

'Welcome to Iceland – only $4 more than the street price back home. I'm glad I bought my three bottles of duty free in Montreal.'

'Three? The exemption is one.'

'For civilians – I'm a poet, a skald in íslensk.'

When we boarded the bus for Reykjavík, Margaret snuggled against me, while Harrison sat in front of us.

'As the bus leaves the terminal building, I want you to observe the sculpture on the right.'

Perched on a pile of rock is a big stainless steel egg which appears to be hatching a pterodactyl chick.

'Not a pterodactyl chick,' Harrison said. 'Look more closely.'

'A Concorde?'

'Got it in one. Now look out the other side of the bus ... across the water, follow those distant mountains to the left as far as the land goes ... see the snow-capped peak at the end?'

'Yes.'

'The mountain range is Snæfellsnes and the white peak is the glacier Snæfellsjökull covering the volcano, and it was through the entrance to that volcano that the travellers began the journey to the centre of the earth in Jules Verne's eponymous novel.'

Margaret snuggled deeper.

'Harrison, shut up – I barely slept on the flight.'

'Utter lack of curiosity, the closed mind of the literary critic,' Harrison sniffed. 'Hopeless. Only one redeeming feature ...'

'Harrison ...'

'Great tits.'

Margaret moaned.

'Or should that be two redeeming features?'

Margaret hit him with her magazine.

Heidi was at the check-in desk of our hotel.

'... yes, I do realize the form says the deposit is non-refundable, but I am with the official Quebec delegation, so it is a matter of diplomatic privilege, surely.'

'Of course, that is a different situation. Could I just see your diplomatic passport?'

'Ahh, well, I am not actually a diplomat myself, but I am in Iceland as a representative, as it were, of the Quebec Government.'

'Then, perhaps you could have the Quebec embassy or consulate get in touch with us, madame. You'll find a telephone over there.'

'Harrison! Will, Margaret! Thank God you're here at last. Perhaps you can explain the ... the anomalies of Quebec.'

'Certainly,' replied Harrison. 'If the young lady will just bring her psychiatrist, her medications, and her witch doctor out to the terrace, we'll be glad to oblige. Drinks on the shrinks, of course.'

'Harrison, be serious for just one minute, will you. I'm worried sick about Marie-Claire, she's gone all strange ...'

'That's a change?'

'Shut up and listen! One minute she's laughing, the next she's weeping, one minute everyone adores her, the next everyone's out to get her, and I'm pretty strung out myself, so anyway she wants me and Guðrún to stay with her over at the Saga, Guðrún's there taking care of her right now, so I came to get our deposit back on our room here, I mean have you seen the price of a cup of coffee?'

'No doubt Marie-Claire can offer you all the diplomatic coffee you want.'

'You should see her suite – it's fabulous. Unlike the rest of this wretched town. What a dump.'

'Ever been to Sorel?'

'Anything beats Sorel. Shit, I'll have to get Marie-Claire on the case, and I don't know if the poor dear can hack it. Anyway, I can't stand here chatting – the limo is waiting.'

As she headed for the door, I asked why she wasn't on our flight.

'And there's another refund I have to get back.'

'You swam?'

'Silly billy – Marie-Claire got us a Quebec government jet.'

Margaret was wide awake by now. 'With free champagne and caviar, no doubt,' she remarked.

'Of course. She didn't want us to have to show our piercings to the security guards. But best of all, sweetie, you should see the bed!'

Margaret is in a deep sleep after a busy day, an expensive evening. After checking in, we napped until early afternoon, then joined Harrison for lunch in the dulcet sunshine of the hotel's rooftop bar with a panorama of downtown Reykjavík, the university, the white spire of Hallgrímskirkja, the silver dome of the Perlan.

Harrison telephoned the university to ask where the conference was being held, and learned the university refused to let the Canada-Scandinavia Association anywhere near the campus, so he asked the woman at the front desk to see if she could discover anything. We were with him an hour before she came with the news.

'The police questioned a group of foreigners last night – several Norwegians, Danes and Swedes. They all claimed they were poets. The police say they are only poets of alcohol, drugs and women.'

'Real poets, then. Did the police learn where the conference is being held?'

'They are not convinced there is a conference, but the drug squad says the foreigners may be operating from a room in a building near the docks.'

'How do we find it?'

She looked at us doubtfully.

'Perhaps if you go to the Kólaportið, the flea market, and ask there.' She showed us on the map.

After ten minutes dodging BMWs and blondes on cellphones, we found the flea market in an old stone office building near the docks. Harrison approached a guy with a nose ring and a display of suggestive smoking paraphernalia.

'I don't know about poets, man, but I think I know the dudes you mean.'

He led us outside and pointed to a dilapidated building.

'Your friends, man, they've got Mountain-grown West Fjord gold, the best shit in Norway.'

The ground floor was a mite dingy, and the upstairs dingier, but the conference room was squalid. A dozen people lounged about, some asleep on derelict furniture, others on the floor. Three half-naked men were urging a half-naked woman to have another toke. At a desk by a window, a bear of a man in baggy clothes was chewing a cigar, tapping at a laptop, and growling into a telephone. He glanced at us and barked in several languages; as one was English I understood he was telling us to do something anatomically impossible.

'Ég snakke ekki norsk, Øystein,' said Harrison. 'Vær så snill, talarðu engelsku?'

The burly man brightened.

'Harrison, you don't know if you're talking norsk og íslensk, but I love you, you horrible, wonderful genius of a Montrealer. Velkominn til Íslands!'

Hugs all around, then Øystein offered us coffee, beer, schnapps, cigars, dope.

'I know,' said Harrison, 'Mountain-grown West Fjord gold, the best shit in Norway. Maybe later, it's barely sunrise in Montreal.'

'Well, perhaps you want to try Sigrid there. She is a Danish poet, very friendly. Even with ladies,' he added to Margaret. 'Just join in.'

'Perhaps another time,' Harrison sniffed.

'You are a snob, my friend,' said Øystein. 'She is the loneliest dew-drop from hell, but I sure make her laugh. Look what she's doing to Sven-Erik – that's real talent.'

'Remarkable. So how's the conference going?'

'The university has not been understanding, but probably the University of Oslo would be just as bad. Universities prefer dead poets.'

'No hospitality, no generosity, no flexibility.'

'Exactly. Anyway, I've already set up readings and concerts and lectures in half a dozen other places – bookstores, bars, parks. I'm doing a reading tonight at ten, maybe sing some songs if Kristian wakes up – he's a fantastic guitar player when he gets his medications balanced. You and your friends absolutely must come. Read some of your poems too. It's in Mál og Menning, the big bookstore on Laugavegur, here, I'll show you on the map ...'

He put an arm across Harrison's shoulders and drew him over to the desk. I thought to examine the view from the window, but found myself stepping in a pool of vomit. Margaret told Harrison we'd wait for him over in the flea market.

Margaret at once saw the crucial point: 'If Marie-Claire really is falling apart, she's going to kill Heidi for getting her into this. Hotel, limo, government jet – it must have cost thousands – and nothing to promote the glory of Quebec!'

'And if the papers at home find out ... She must have brought a press attaché with her, perhaps even some reporters.'

'Oh, that won't be a problem – the Quebec press is supine. Marie-Claire could bang the president on the front steps of the Alþingi at high noon and they'd report that she had offered a profound gesture of respect to the independent people of Iceland from the soon-to-be-independent people of Quebec. No, she'll be worried about other ministers using it to knife her.'

'Her own colleagues?'

'They're politicians – betrayal is part of the job description.'

Harrison rejoined us.

'Øystein tells me that around the corner one can find the best hot dogs in Iceland. If they are, they'll be fine indeed, because hot dogs are one of the culinary glories of the country. In the fast food category.'

'The further I get from the conference, the happier I'll be.'

'Don't let appearances deceive you, Megs – some of Øystein's mob may be a bit louche, but he himself is not a man, he's a force of nature – he's already published over thirty books – mainly poetry, but also short stories, three novels, translations, and his second CD – blues in English – is just out.'

'Over thirty? Can any of them be any good?'

'I don't read much Norwegian, but the stuff I've seen in translation is good, yes. As for the conference, he has already rescheduled nearly all the events – here's the agenda he printed out for us. See, you and the brigadier are booked for the Nordic House two days from now, very respectable. What the hell, the three of us liberated some school money, we add a line to the CV, and we get to enjoy Iceland. I suggest we do a bit of light sightseeing and shopping, then find a bar and have a serious academic discussion about ...'

'About the legal position of three Canadians arrested for possession and trafficking?'

'Megs, there's none so puritanical as the reformed. Øystein got an arts grant from the Norwegian government, but most of these other poets are broke, so they're trying to pay their way by spreading a little happiness.'

'Maybe we can implicate Marie-Claire in the drugs.'

'Don't try, Brigadier – she'd grab all the profits, shop the lot of us, and come out of it with a medal.'

After the hot dogs – which we recommend without reservation – we stopped at the post office for stamps and airmail stickers for post cards, then shopped. Margaret was soon adept at converting kroner into dollars – 'at that price, this shawl must be woven with real gold thread.' Harrison and I quickly lost interest, but Margaret consulted several women, then led us a few blocks to a shop offering Icelandic craft work.

'The prices are decent,' she admitted after a few minutes of scrutiny. 'Odd thing – the designs seem as Celtic as they are Icelandic. But these earrings, Harrison – your daughters would love them. I know it's early to think about Christmas, but if you don't get them now, you'll be kicking yourself in December.'

Harrison was at first reluctant, but we left with bags of jewellery, runic tea towels and T-shirts, maps, and books on local birds and the Icelandic horse.

'Enough of this energetic virtue, Megs. I'm exhausted and parched. That Hotel Borg on the square looked gracious enough even for you.'

We whiled away a few hours in restored nineteenth-century elegance sipping drinks, comparing our purchases, looking through the guide book, and musing on the other buildings on the square – the small cathedral and the Alþingi, the parliament.

'Have you noticed the name of this beer?' asked Harrison. 'Of course you haven't. *Egils Gull* means *Egil's Gold*. That's the great one himself, as you can see from the name of the brewery – Ölgerðin Egill Skallagrímsson. This is a country for warrior poets:

> 'A languid love for lilies did not blight him!
> Lank limbs and haggard cheeks did not delight him!

'His grandfather Ulf was called Kveldulf, the Night-Wolf, reputedly a shape-shifter. Egil was a rough boy – at seven, he buried an axe in the head of a playmate. He grew into the ugliest, most dangerous man in Iceland. Among his descendants was Snorri Sturluson, who was not only a great writer and the likely author of *Egil's Saga*, but was the lögsögumaður, the law speaker, president of the Alþingi, though it wasn't in that building over there, it was out at a place called Þingvellir. I'm talking about a thousand years ago.'

Margaret snapped her fingers.

'An ancient parliament – that's it! Marie-Claire is here because she wants to show how absurd it is that Iceland, with a quarter of a million inhabitants, is a flourishing independent country with its own language, while Quebec, with five million, is still groaning under the yoke of Anglo-Canadian imperialism. Heidi must take Marie-Claire to Þingvellir – it will even look good on her expense claim.'

'Megs, you are, as always, a genius. And I think we might go along as well. My treat – I shall rent a car.'

'I hope your mortgage is paid off.'

'I'll sell Faith, Hope and Charity to white slavers.'

'Sure, and they can apprentice with Julia,' said Margaret.

Interesting, this allusion to her evening work – all three of us laughed knowingly. Margaret dropped the remark with aplomb, and I found I felt comfortable, even privileged to share her secret.

Surely the time difference in this direction should have me sleeping in; but unaccountably I was up at six and did the above account of yesterday afternoon. I'm not sure I can remember all the details of the remains of the day. Back to the hotel to get rid of our purchases; freshen up; to a restaurant called Við Tjönina for a dinner of hakarl, puffin, lamb and whale meat; refusal to contemplate the cost of dinner in Canadian dollars; pub crawl which only just missed being a literal crawl.

'Hadn't we better get in touch with Heidi?' I suggested as we sat in Fógetinn, a homey bar in the oldest building in Reykjavík.

'Don't worry, Brigadier Ass, downtown Reykjavík is small enough that we're sure to bump into her.'

So we were not surprised to see a limousine parked in front of the Café Paris, and the Minister of the Weeping Soul of the People in Chains and her entourage through the open patio doors.

'Wait,' said Margaret, 'you guys had better not go in. This may be Reykjavík, but if Marie-Claire sees a couple of têtes carrées she'll really freak out.'

'Okay, Megs, but stay away from the two knuckle-draggers in the Hawaiian shirts – they're doughnut dragoons.'

When Heidi and Guðrún joined us, Margaret explained about the excursion to Þingvellir.

'Brilliant, Maggie, but Guðrún has already set up a trip to this Thingie place.'

'And then to see the geysers,' said Guðrún.

'Poor dear Marie-Claire is in ecstasy!'

'She's on that now, is she?' Margaret murmured to me.

'And Harrison, Guðrún says you're to be part of it.'

'I'm doomed.'

'We're all doomed,' and burst into tears. 'Shit, there goes the mascara! Yes, we're all doomed,' giggling, 'Guðrún says we're going to be immortalized or something, don't you dear?'

'It's all part of the prophecy.'

'Tell me when and where this is to happen,' said Harrison, 'so I can be somewhere else.'

'Oh,' replied Guðrún, 'there's no avoiding it – just carry on with whatever you have planned and the prophecy will bring everyone together – I've heard the runes singing their wisdom.'

'And we are off to a bookstore to hear a Norwegian singing his wisdom.'

'Ohh, must rush,' squeaked Heidi, 'we ladies have such teeny-tiny bladders!'

Margaret frowned after her. 'She's as off the rails as Marie-Claire.'

Canadian bookstores could do worse than copy the practices of Mál og Menning. Not only does it carry books and magazines in half a dozen languages, it was still in full operation when we arrived at ten. The upstairs lounge where Øystein performed serves espresso and pastries, but also beer and wine. The great man himself beckoned us over, sat us at his table, and introduced us to the stunning blonde seated beside him.

'Þordis was Miss Iceland a few years ago,' he explained as he embraced her.

Þordis seemed to be all blonde hair, black mini-dress and legs.

'He exaggerates,' she said with a British accent, 'I was only a runner-up.'

'Don't be fooled,' said Øystein, 'Þordis is more than just a pretty face – she appreciates poetry – and poets, especially Norwegian poets.' He stood up. 'Now I would play on Satan's trumpet.'

He kissed Þordis's cheek then made his way to the podium.

'Do you understand Norwegian?' Þordis asked.

'Unfortunately, no,' Margaret replied.

'He's very good. Perhaps you will sense it from the sound. I'll translate a bit, but I don't want to talk while he's reading. I think he's going to sing a few in English from his new CD.'

Øystein would have been impressive reading in any language. I'm not sure how much the Icelanders understood, but they gave him a standing ovation when he was done.

Þordis smiled at us and murmured, 'Now I must join Øystein – promise you will not laugh at me.'

'We promise.'

'Do you know how many languages she speaks?' Margaret asked when Þordis was out of earshot.

'Did I hear her say four?'

'English, German, Norwegian and French, and that's not counting Icelandic. And she can get along in Danish, Swedish, Italian and Spanish. She has a PhD in linguistics from Exeter. Not just a pretty face indeed.'

'There's Guðrún.'

'Grab the glasses.'

After picking up the chair and wiping whipped cream from the man's pants, Guðrún joined us.

'Why didn't you bring the Banger Sisters?' Harrison asked.

'Heidi had to sedate Marie-Claire and take her back to the hotel.'

'Good.'

'At least they're not in jail.'

'Begin at the beginning, child.'

'Well, Marie-Claire insisted that in a place called the Café Paris she should be able to talk French to the waiter. Of course, the waiter did speak French, but Parisian French, so he couldn't understand a word Marie-Claire was saying.'

'The Montreal accent is a bit obscure.'

'Then he got the other waiters to try her in Russian and Finnish and Hungarian and so on, and Marie-Claire had hysterics, so her bodyguards beat up the waiters, and they were trashing the bar when the police arrested them – the bodyguards, not Heidi and Marie-Claire – so I came here.'

'And how, Miss Snæfellsnes, did you find us? More Saab, Volvo prophecy?'

'When you said it was in a bookstore, I knew it must be this one.'

'Common sense,' said Margaret.

I heard Guðrún say softly, 'But it's is all part of the prophecy, I know it is.'

Kristian had apparently achieved chemical harmony, because he provided fine accompaniment as Øystein growled out half a dozen of his own blues numbers in Norwegian and English, with Þordis weaving her soprano above his gravelly baritone.

'Not a man,' Margaret remarked to Harrison, 'but a force of nature.'

'If you're that impressed, Megs, why not buy his CDs?'

'I already have my credit card in my hand.'

'And now Øystein is taking me to the best jazz joint in Reykjavík – are you game?'

'I'm afraid poets have more stamina than academics.'

As we reached the turning of the stairs, I glanced back and saw

Guðrún talking with Øystein, Kristian, and Þordis – what now?

But I hear Margaret stirring. Just coming on eight o'clock, and the sun is bright in a clear blue sky. We are favoured.

Twenty-Four

Two words would comprehend my future – *death* and *hell*.

Oh dear, dear! What mun we have next? Master, master, our young lady –

The contents of the pan began to boil.

The little dog was yelping in the garden yet.

I lingered round them, under that benign sky; watched the moths fluttering among the heath and harebells; listened to the soft wind breathing through the grass; and wondered how anyone could ever imagine unquiet slumbers for the sleepers in that quiet earth.

Because of the events of that day, we have been interviewed by the Reykjavík *Morgunbladið*, *The Times*, the *New York Times*, *Le Monde* and *Der Spiegel*, to name but a few. CNN, preoccupied with the anniversary of September 11, has finally stopped pestering us.

But the exposure has had benefits. After three years as a junior language instructor at the University of Iceland, Þordis has won a full professorship at Princeton, as well as modelling contracts with Gianfranco Ferré and Alexander McQueen; Steven Spielberg is speculating that Indiana Jones may have a younger sister. Øystein and Kristian have signed for six CDs with Virgin Records; the first, *Geysir!* is due out for the Christmas market. Because of her beguiling appearances on the cover of *National Geographic* and in its televison special, Guðrún has been hired by Ken Burns for a series on the immigrant experience. She is on leave from the college.

Lacking the beauty and accomplishments of the others, I have returned to pedagogic obscurity. Only Margaret, for reasons I need not go into, avoided the cameras and had us say she was in Reykjavík that day.

« 181 »

But the combined resources of the world media did not suffice to winkle from us the full story, not as it happened, not the nuances.

After breakfast, we walked to a car rental agency near the city air terminal. Harrison insisted on paying, but had Margaret registered as the first driver.

'Harrison, you know Iceland – you navigate.'

'The last time I was here I spent most of my time up the coast around Borgarnes, Egil's home territory. Here, Brigadier, you take this stuff.'

I studied the maps.

'Þingvellir is not far east of here. Straight up Hringbraut, then follow the signs for Mosfellsbær.'

'Mosfellsbær? Egil lived out his last years at Mosfell farm. In fact, he died there, and was finally buried there. We must stop and pay our respects.'

'Can we do it on the way back? I'm not sure about the roads outside the city, so I can't tell how long this trip will take.'

'No respect. Critics.'

He lapsed into silence. Margaret and I were cheerful, even giddy as we took the freeway past steel and smoked glass office blocks, through prosperous suburbs, then out into the countryside, that strange land of mountain and heath, pasture and moonscape. In under an hour the hills to our right fell away to reveal Þingvellavatn – Thingvellir Lake – spreading away to the south. We found we were on a plateau, and had to drive to the north end of the escarpment where a road branched off and descended to the valley floor.

'Stop here, Margaret, and I'll tell you what the guidebook says.'

'Typical – you accept a guy's proposal of marriage and the next thing he's ordering you about.'

'Silence, woman. Now, we are at the apex of a triangle which widens down to the lake. The triangle is the Þingvellahraun, the Thingvellir Lava Field. The Alþingi was held at the base of that escarpment to the west. I might add that the escarpment is the edge of the North American tectonic plate, while those hills to the left are the edge of the European tectonic plate ... '

'We're sitting on a seam of the earth?'

'We are, indeed, Harrison, and further down we'll see some actual cracks left as the two plates pull away from one another.'

'But I left Quebec because I was afraid of falling though the cracks. I should have stayed in a bar. Or in Mosfell.'

'Stop whining. Drive on, Margaret.'

Because Heidi and Marie-Claire came through here several hours after us, some of the television coverage included shots of Þingvellir. What television couldn't show, of course, was the awe Þingvellir inspires. Harrison was obviously moved. He muttered about Egil and Snorri and Njál, then wandered off. Margaret and I sauntered along the base of the escarpment, listened to the waterfall, gazed down into the crystal blue water of the fissures. We smiled, we shook our heads in wonder, we kissed.

As we drove eastward across the lava plain, Harrison was gazing back toward the escarpment.

'From your map, how far to Gullfoss?' Margaret asked.

'An hour, hour and a half, depending on the roads.'

'Perhaps we'll see a place for lunch.'

'Sounds good to me.'

'Harrison?'

Margaret raised her eyebrows to me.

'Harrison?'

We took his silence for consent, and half an hour later stopped at a shop in a village. We ate our shrimp sandwiches at a shaded table behind the shop, musing on the golden fields of grain spreading southward to the distant hills, all shimmering in the heat.

At last, Harrison lifted his beer.

'To Egil Skallagrímsson. To Egil and all the skalds, the serious poets.'

'To Egil,' we said.

'Egil was a naughty man. Spent his best years looting and pillaging northern Europe. His most famous exploit came after he was captured by his bitter enemy, Eirík Bloodaxe, the King of York. "Gotcha, you son of a bitch," said Eirík, "you die at sunrise." Egil replied, "Fair enough, Eirík, and I'd gladly do the same for you, you wanker, you despoiler of boys' bottoms, you debaucher of livestock. But I'll offer you a deal – by sunrise I'll compose a poem in praise of you, the finest, most intricate, most subtle, most delicate piece of skaldic verse you or anyone has ever heard. If it pleases you, you will set me free and let me go home, alive and unharmed, to Iceland." Egil was as good as his word, and Eirík Bloodaxe was as good as his. The poem is no slight ditty – it's something like a hundred and twenty lines long, and is known as the *Höfuðlausn*, the "head ransom", and you can read it today, if you read medieval Icelandic, which isn't much different from modern Icelandic.'

'Thank you, Professor Morgan, for this informative lecture.'

'I tell my students they'll learn something in every class of mine.'

'I learned the colourful dialogue which was not included in the saga itself. In fact, as I recall, Egil was silent during the confrontation, his friend Arinbjorn did the talking, and Eirík spoke less than his wife Gunnhild who hated Egil even more than Eirík did.'

'Megs, that's the point – Egil was silent, he didn't bandy words with the angry and the vindictive. In the morning, he spoke as a poet should – in poetry.'

'Excuse me, Harrison – are you saying you're a superficial bore?'

'Exactly. Mine has been a botched life. Egil was a skald, I'm a wanker. Hell, I'm not even a wanker – these twenty years I've been a thing of shreds and patches, a scribbler of verse, of doggerel, of drivel, not even up to Sir WSG on a bad day. But now I share something with Egil in his eighties when he was living at Mosfell. He was blind and going deaf, so that the women on the farm laughed at him as he stumbled about. He spoke a poem about his feebleness:

> 'Vals hefk váfur helsis;
> váfallr em ek skalla;
> blautr erum bergis fótar
> borr, en hlust es þnorrin.

'I'll have to pass over the kennings, but a literal translation gives something like:

> 'My neck is in doubt,
> I'm likely to fall on my pate,

Wet is my foot that
Bores, and my ears are dry.

'It's poignant with evocations of the great man he once was and the tragic-comic dodderer he has become.'

'Foot that bores?'

'You'll understand from my free translation:

'Neck unstrung,
Balance tilted,
Hammer unhung,
Ears silted.'

'He's saying he is impotent?'

'As am I.'

'What!'

'Obviously you didn't read *Egil's Saga* carefully enough – it's quite clear, though it's only a line.'

'Idiot! I meant you!'

'Sorry to spoil the party, Megs – you have doubtless been expecting me to exercise my droit de seigneur on your nuptial night, but I am become but a spectator at the great game.'

'You bastard – why didn't you tell me?'

'Never mind the why and wherefore – I suppose I wanted you to choose the brigadier on your own. If you'd known, you'd always have wondered if you'd accepted him because I'd passed my best-before date, not because you loved him.'

'But you're the stud muffin of Westmount! Wives tingle, husbands tremble, daughters drool ...'

'Slander!'

'Your reputation ...'

'Reputation, reputation, reputation! O, I have lost my reputation! I have lost the immortal part of myself, and what remains is incapable of being bestial. Yes, well, mine was always something of a bubble reputation, more honoured in the breach than in the observance.'

'But ...'

'It's all ancient history.'

'You've fathered three daughters!'

'Exactly – from seed sown during the first and second Reagan administrations. In any case, the departure of wife-four-and-a-half took the wind from the wings of my falcon – to use a kenning of sorts. And if you wonder about my talent as a poet, you might reflect on the rhetorical dog's breakfast I've been laying before you. And don't bother suggesting Viagra – I've tried it. Oysters avail not. In the cause of animal rights and the politically correct, I'll forgo powdered rhinoceros horn, pickled bear's liver, salted tiger penis, and other remedies favoured, allegedly, in the Orient. Spells cast by Miss Tectonic Fissure have been ineffectual. I shall also forgo psychiatry, psychoanalysis, group therapy for geldings, male bonding, the Limp Dicks Hang Together Support Group, Eunuchs Anonymous, capons.com, and all other forms of voodoo – they're more likely to render my toothless muse menopausal than to rejuvenate me.'

'You're not joking about this, are you?'

'Even the Savoy operas, however topsy-turvy, yield the truth at last.'

Margaret reached for his hand.

'Harrison, I'm sorry to hear it.'

'Oh, don't feel sorry for me, Megs – after more than thirty years of mano-a-mano and groino-a-groino in the battles of the sexes, I find I am happy enough in retirement, remembering a darkling bed swept with confused alarms of struggle and flight, where ignorant lovers clash by night. And what did marriage get me? Egil's final jest involved a bag of silver – for the ex-wives I'm just a bag of silver to be yelled at. No, the crucial question is – what about the poetry? If I could make the poetry live, I could live. Egil wrote the *Höfuðlausn* not *as if* his life depended upon it, but *because* his life depended on it.'

'What are you proposing – to kill yourself if *The New Yorker* doesn't publish your next limerick?'

'I'm not sure. Perhaps I shall assassinate Heidi or Marie-Claire – what would Egil have thought of them?'

'They're harmless!'

'Marie-Claire? Did you hear her latest? After the blue tattoo craze crashed and burned, she suggested castrating all Anglo baby boys and transplanting their gonads to French boys so they'd have better odds of having babies – *Four balls – take your base!*'

'It wasn't to French baby boys – it was baby girls, so they could impregnate themselves – and it was a joke.'

'She can have mine if she wants them.'

'Marie-Claire is just silly and excitable. Like shaking a can of warm Pepsi.'

'Megs!'

'What now?'

'Or perhaps Heidi would like them for her mantelpiece ...'

'Never mind, Will, inadvertent political incorrectness. And Heidi really is rather sweet. She's trying so hard to be a woman that even I forget sometimes.'

Harrison muttered but didn't disagree. 'In any case,' he added, 'I shall retire from the college. So, young Will, I promote you – you are now the very model of a modern major general.'

'Retire? That is certainly taking your life in your own hands.'

'More effective than taking myself in my own hands. And don't be sarcastic, Margaret – I'm serious.'

'But how will you live? Isn't your pension lower if you quit before sixty-five?'

'Money is crass – don't talk of it. This is not about anything as bourgeois as a Hippo pension – it's about life, about poetry. Finished with your sandwiches? Then let's go – I want to see this Gullfoss. Now, you'll have guessed that because *Egils Gull* means *Egil's Gold*, *Gullfoss* means *Golden Waterfall* so ...'

Along the way we passed Geysir, but because of the many tour buses decided to stop on the way back.

'Anyway,' I informed them after looking at the guidebook, 'It seems Geysir is not what it was. Earthquakes in 1294 started it, but it fell dormant in 1915. Then from June 17, 2000, Independence Day, a series of earthquakes got it going again, though it's neither as regular nor as spectacular as it used to be – only a few times a day, and only up to eight or ten metres.'

'How apt,' said Harrison from the back seat, 'Egil and I both personified in Iceland's most famous tourist attraction: *Hey sir, Geysir, you can no longer get it up, sir.*'

'*Geysir* rhyming with *Hey sir* is the correct pronunciation, by the way.'

'A perfect rhyme. I'll use it. No, I'll not use it – that's all over. No more doggerel.'

'Bravo, Harrison,' said Margaret.

'Do you know how I get through every day of my life? Have done for ten years?'

'Australian Shiraz? Islay straight malt?'

'No, I have a little mantra – *Nothing – hope for nothing, ask for nothing, expect nothing, you are nothing.* Keep your eyes on the road, Megs – I tell you nothing you couldn't have guessed.'

'Harrison, stop, you mustn't talk like this!'

'No? Think of Egil facing Eirík Bloodaxe.'

'Stop! This is ridiculous, grotesque!'

'Isn't that a sign for Gullfoss, keep left?'

As we climbed the long stairway back to the parking lot, Margaret said, 'I wonder if Heidi and Marie-Claire got out to Þingvellir.'

'At least Guðrún would know the way.'

'If they took Guðrún with them, we'd have felt the earthquake.'

'Who's got the camera?' said Harrison. 'Take a picture of me with the falls in the background: "I'm at Gullfoss and you're not – nyah-nyah!" Make sure you get the rainbow. Snaps for the Three Graces – they can put them in the blue box after I'm gone.'

'Harrison, stop it!'

'Habits are hard to break, Megs.' He held up a finger and looked steadily at each of us in turn. 'I mean that about the photos – see that you take care of that – take care of things ... the girls.'

'What do you mean, Harrison?'

Her tone, her grip on my arm indicated Margaret's agitation.

'Just get a print for each of them, if you would, please. Now then, General ...'

'Harrison!'

'... would you kindly consult your guidebook and suggest something else around here worth seeing until it's time to go back to Geysir?'

He was not going to discuss it further. I looked at the map.

'We'd never make it down to Njal's Saga country and back. Hekla seems to be about an hour southeast, probably beyond those hills over there, but the guidebook says the peak is almost always hidden in cloud.'

The bright sunshine encouraged us, and we had plenty of time, so we drove off, hoping to catch a glimpse of the volcano medieval Europeans considered the mouth of hell, but it was indeed obscured.

'Another personification of yours truly,' said Harrison. 'An extinct volcano with its head in the clouds.'

'It's not extinct – its most recent eruption was in 1991.'

'So was mine, Major General Ass, so was mine.'

We arrived back at Geysir as the last tour buses were departing and the souvenir barn was closing, so we had no trouble parking. Indeed, we were alone as we crossed the road and climbed the barren slope toward the welling hot pools and smoking fissures, toward Geysir, and Strokkur, the smaller but most reliable geyser.

With a great whoosh, Strokkur threw a plume of water skyward. Harrison, standing near it, beckoned us over.

'The sign says it'll blow again in eight minutes or so. You might as well take a snap of me next time. For the Three Graces, you understand. An emblem of erstwhile fatherhood.'

'Smell the sulphur.'

'Brimstone – another emblem of me.'

'You'll never forgive Hekla for hiding itself.'

'Surely that's *herself*.'

Geysir was indeed a sad sight – a steaming azure pool inside a roped-off circle about twenty metres across. From time to time, water welled above the mouth in a frothing dome, then subsided into uneasy calm.

Margaret and I climbed to an outcrop on a hill above the thermal area, while Harrison wandered off by himself. The view, as at lunch, was across vast fields of grain toward distant grey and brown hills. The sun, behind the hills to our right, would be granting us twilight for some hours yet, and the full moon was rising before us.

'Will, do you remember I told you Guðrún declared my secret to Harrison?'

'Yes.'

'And Harrison changed the subject by asking what his was?'

'She said he was impotent. How do you suppose she knew?'

'Not with runic mumbo-jumbo. But I'm worried about him – he's almost as upset as Heidi and Marie-Claire.'

'Oh, look, down by the restaurant – a limo, the same one we saw last night, I think.'

The driver opened the door and three people got out.

'Yes, that's them.'

'What in heaven's name are they wearing?'

'Not trekking togs, certainly.'

Marie-Claire was in the blue leather pants she'd worn on the Tour de l'isle, though now she also wore the matching jacket. Heidi sported a tight spaghetti-strap top and blue miniskirt, and Guðrún was draped in a hooded black mantle. Despite the August heat, she seemed to be wearing boots and gloves. Guðrún raised a staff and led them across the road. Marie-Claire stumbled as they began their way up the slope.

'Heidi is almost carrying Marie-Claire – she's sedated or stoned.'

'Should we go down and speak to them?' I wondered.

'They don't know we're here, and they don't know our car. Let's let them be.'

'Where's Harrison?'

'I haven't seen him for ten minutes.'

'Perhaps he slipped away to the restaurant for a drink.'

'No, look down there – in the shadows behind that hillock. And aren't Øystein, Þordis and Kristian with him?'

'Guðrún must have had them come earlier.'

In the moonlight, our dull clothes hid us. In any case, the three women seemed intent on what they were doing – toking up. They paused as Strokkur erupted, then walked on toward the pool of Geysir.

Strikingly erect as ever, Guðrún stood facing Geysir with the full moon directly behind her; she motioned the other two, now hand in hand, to stand on the other side of Geysir facing her and the moon.

Guðrún stepped up onto a rock, turned toward the moon and raised her staff. Bits of words drifted in the stillness.

'I've got it,' I said, 'Guðrún is performing some sort of marriage ceremony!'

'Whatever it is, it's something straight out of the head of Guðrún Sigurdardóttir under the influence, something appropriately flaky. You're right – Heidi is carrying a bouquet. It's all rather touching.'

'Where's the camera?'

'No, it's not a bouquet, it's Tinker Bell!'

Neither of us noticed Harrison approaching until just before he joined the group.

Now what?

Margaret lowered the camera.

Harrison took a few tokes, then held out his hands to the bridal couple.

'They're giving him the rings,' Margaret whispered. 'He's going to be ring bearer, father of the brides, bridesmaid, and best man, all in one.'

'He did say he wanted to do something with his life.'

Margaret giggled. 'But he's been married, so I suppose he's a matron of honour, not a bridesmaid.'

When we heard the guitar we turned and saw Øystein, Þordis, and Kristian standing in the moonlight on top of their hillock. At that distance and in the open air, their words were indistinct, but the tone was clear enough – a strange, melancholic keening.

Guðrún continued with her incantation. Marie-Claire stumbled again, sank to her knees; Heidi and Harrison caught her, lifted her, Heidi held her in her arms. Harrison stood at attention behind them. Guðrún turned, and Harrison held his hands toward her. She took the rings and put them on Heidi's and Marie-Claire's fingers.

'The bride kissed the bride,' said Margaret, 'and the newlyweds departed in smiles for their honeymoon in exotic Reykjavík.'

Heidi set Tinker Bell on the ground.

'No, look – they're ...'

Still holding Marie-Claire, Heidi stepped to the edge of Geysir's pool. Suddenly she splashed into the pool, held Marie-Claire tight, then leapt into the steaming centre. In a moment they disappeared beneath the surface.

'That water's boiling!'

'Margaret! Harrison too!'

He gave a brief major general's salute, waved his hand in dismissal or resignation, then leapt and disappeared as well.

Margaret was on her feet and running, stumbling down the slope with me after her.

'Guðrún! Guðrún, what have you done?' Margaret screamed.

Guðrún stepped over the rope and walked toward us, lighting another joint. Her costume, now that we saw it better, was obviously meant to evoke historic Icelandic motifs. The black hooded mantle was adorned with jewels, and a purse hung from a belt of linked metal figures. Her leather bootlaces were tipped with pewter knobs which glinted in the moonlight. Her staff was topped with brass set with jewels.

'Tinker Bell – come, Tinks!'

But the pathetic blue dog remained within the ropes, rushing back and forth, whimpering and yipping.

Guðrún motioned us back.

'Tinks will come – animals sense the rhythms of nature better than we do, but we can't take any chances – that water's really hot, and I don't know how far the spray will go. Here, have some weed – I got it from Øystein's friends – it's fantastic stuff.'

Margaret grabbed her and shook her.

'Never mind the dope, Guðrún, what have you done?'

Under the white-lined hood, Guðrún's shaved head looked ominously skull-like.

'Take your hands off me, Margaret, I'm a sacred völva.'

'You've murdered them!'

'No, it was their fate. Surely it's obvious – the world is too narrow and stupid to accept them, so they've united in marriage, and now they've united themselves to the elements of earth, air, water and fire. We'd best stand even further back. Oh, good, you have a camera – make sure you get a shot of it the first time.'

'What are you babbling about?'

'It's all explained by the runes carved into my staff.' She held it before us. 'Oh, of course, you don't understand runes. But look at them.'

We stared with incomprehension at the spiky characters.

'And Øystein and Þordis are singing ward songs – she taught him the words – they attract the spirits to the seiður.'

'But why?'

'You know that Geysir was dormant for nearly a hundred years?'

'Yes, but ...'

'And it revived a bit after the earthquakes two years ago?'

'Yes ...'

'On June 17, Icelandic Independence Day! Is that an omen or is that an omen?'

'An omen of what – another Quebec referendum?'

'Be sarcastic if you want, Margaret, but these runes spell out an ancient Icelandic prophecy – *Geysir lives on the hard, the soft, the bitter.* Which means bone, grease and acid.'

'More likely they say *Björk rules.*'

'You'll see the proof in a few minutes. Geysir the Great will live again. All the remaining debris is going to be cleared out by the sacrifice of those three wonderful people. Þor will see that they go straight to Valhalla.'

'Þor? Valhalla? Guðrún, you're mad!'

'Am I? Can't you feel the earth trembling?'

She pointed her staff toward the pool of Geysir. The tremble was slight, but perceptible. With it came a rumbling, deep and low, but loud enough that it covered the music from the hillock.

'See, Harrison provides the bone, Heidi the fat and Marie-Claire the acid.'

'Nonsense – you didn't even know Harrison was here.'

'Of course I knew – I'm a völva.'

Margaret paused, released Guðrún, for Geysir the Great was rumbling louder, the mouth roiling, boiling, welling up, first a dome of foaming water, then a rock flying skyward, then stuttering spurts of water and gravel and boulders in a fan as big as a house. A pause as the spray subsided, but we found it was raining on us a film of thick yellow liquor, a stagnant sickening oil, so that we ran further away in disgust, in fear, in awe.

The little dog with the blue fleur-de-lys on its back leapt up and down, yipping in lost, sad, unknowing rage at the fluttering plume – brown, then beige, then pure white in the moonlight.

But the rumbling and trembling grew under that benign sky; then a roaring column hurtled upward, the crest out of sight far above us, the earth vomiting the debris of centuries, vomiting the remains of those three into the soft wind, and I wondered how anyone could ever imagine quiet slumbers for the sleepers drizzling down on that unquiet earth.

BURT COVIT

Ray Smith was born in Mabou, Nova Scotia, a village on the west coast of Cape Breton. Since 1968, he has lived in Montreal, where he teaches English literature at Dawson College.

His first book, a collection of stories entitled *Cape Breton Is the Thought Control Centre of Canada* (1969) is widely acknowledged as a milestone of early Canadian postmodernism. His other works include *Lord Nelson Tavern, Century, A Night at the Opera* (which won the QSPELL Hugh MacLennan Prize for Fiction) and most recently *The Man Who Loved Jane Austen*.